PENGUIN CRIME FICTION

THE 120-HOUR CLOCK

Francis M. Nevins, Jr., is a professor of law at St. Louis University. He is, as well, an Edgar-winning author (for his *Royal Bloodline: Ellery Queen, Author and Detective*) and the creator of the Loren Mensing novels (whose protagonist makes a brief appearance in this current book). He has published numerous short stories, many of them featuring Milo Turner, but this is Turner's first full-length adventure.

The
120-Hour
Clock

Francis M. Nevins, Jr.

PENGUIN BOOKS

PENGUIN BOOKS

Viking Penguin Inc., 40 West 23rd Street,
New York, New York 10010, U.S.A.
Penguin Books Ltd, 27 Wrights Lane, London W8 5TZ
(Publishing & Editorial) and Harmondsworth,
Middlesex, England (Distribution & Warehouse)
Penguin Books Australia Ltd, Ringwood,
Victoria, Australia
Penguin Books Canada Limited, 2801 John Street,
Markham, Ontario, Canada L3R 1B4
Penguin Books (N.Z.) Ltd, 182–190 Wairau Road,
Auckland 10, New Zealand

First published in the United States of America by
the Walker Publishing Company, Inc., 1986
Published in Penguin Books 1987

All the characters and events portrayed in this story are fictitious.

LIBRARY OF CONGRESS CATALOGING IN PUBLICATION DATA
Nevins, Francis M.
The 120-hour clock.
I. Title.   II. Title: One hundred twenty-hour clock.
PS3564.E854A613   1987   813'.54   87-10602
ISBN 0 14 01.0504 2

Printed in the United States of America by
Offset Paperback Mfrs., Inc., Dallas, Pennsylvania
Set in Times Roman

For the other toads of Toad Hall:
Patty and Pussy Willow and Tar Baby

The 120-Hour Clock

ONE

Why choose such a lunatic life? Why keep so many identities in the air like a mad juggler with his spinning plates? Maybe it's my way of cheating death: if I can live dozens of lives but have to die only once, haven't I pulled off the ultimate existential scam?

Maybe I'm just shy.

From the notebooks of Milo Turner

The word went out from North Jersey and crossed the Hudson on phone lines that were checked for bugs three times a day, and filtered down through various layers of impolite society in the boroughs of the City of New York. There was a certain municipal councilman in one of those Jersey bedroom communities who was desperate to connect with some nationally ranked hit person and lay thirty or forty thousand bills on such a gentleman or lady, if he or she in return would blow away a certain other municipal councilman, who showed signs of being about to crack under prosecutorial pressure and sing a song of corrupt politicos. When I first heard about it I didn't even pretend I was politely curious. I was enjoying one of my extended sabbaticals in Manhattan, a quiet but satisfying round of concerts, art exhibits, movies, and ballet, and reading improving literature and patronizing fine restaurants and dallying with cool slim women, and I hadn't the smallest intention of shelving my pleasures and going back to work.

"But Milo—er, George, this fat fish is practically *begging* you to hook him!" The monkeylike little man at the other end of the decorator sofa in my Central Park South high-rise condo tonged another ice cube into his third water-glassful of my Johnnie Walker Red and downed the drink in one gulp as a sort of protest against my obstinacy.

"But Louie—er, Minky, I don't need the money, and I had an excellent Angler's Platter for dinner just a few nights ago." Minky looked devastated, from which I deduced that he needed a finder's fee badly. Under his birth name Louis Quackenbush and his usual nom de guerre of Lou the Q, he was wanted by federal and state authorities on enough charges to fill a filing cabinet, and he'd been underground as Minky Leach for the past year and a half. He was, I hoped and prayed, the only person in New York who knew my true name and current whereabouts. To the rest of the city I wanted dearly to remain George Boyd, wealthy fortyish culture vulture.

Before he slunk out of the building the little weasel had borrowed two hundred from me that I knew I'd never see again.

The next day's mail brought a humongous assessment from the condominium association for my share of the cost of a new roof for the building, and I decided that perhaps I'd better take a break from leisure and go back to work.

Creating a new identity is easy, if you know the best document forger in the free world. I did. His name is Lafferty, his base is a brownstone on Minetta Street in

Greenwich Village, and I'd done business with him dozens of times. A few visits to his establishment and I was transformed, on paper anyway, into yet another thing I am not, namely a professional eliminator. Armed with these credentials I cautiously let word drift back across the Hudson that I might be interested in talking contract. It took a week to set up the first meet and two weeks more before the politico and I powwowed again. He was short, squat, balding, beetle-browed, and looked so much like the stereotype of a slimy city official that I marveled he had the guts to live the part. At the end of the second meet he said he thought we had a deal but he'd get back to me again to make it final.

Nine days later, a balmy mid-May Friday, he phoned and invited me to dine with him that evening at a place a dozen miles or so from the community in whose governmental offices he served with pride. So as the long day drew down I snagged a cab in front of the Central Park South condo and rode a mile south and a couple of blocks west to the brick fortress of the Port Authority Building and caught a Maplewood Equipment Company 35E to Rochelle Park, New Jersey. I had to dash up the escalator from the ticket windows to catch the next bus and didn't have time to buy an evening paper.

As twilight fell I was sipping Chablis in a booth at the Fireside Inn, an unpretentious culinary paradise on Passaic Street close to the Rochelle Park–Maywood border, and promising myself the pleasure of a return visit at some other time in more desirable company. Blubberbutt slurped liquor like a kid just learning to drink from a glass and shoveled groceries into his mouth like a railroad fireman stoking the engine on a prediesel train. "It's good that we have a meal together," he mumbled through Swedish meatballs from the appetizer buffet. "To close on an arrangement to take a human life, there should be a ritual. The Church is wise. All the

3

important times in life there oughtta be a ritual." He belched. Then he struggled out of his red plush seat and waddled away for his third religious pilgrimage to the appetizer cart.

That was when I reached across the table for the evening paper he'd brought with him to the Inn.

I had nothing in mind whatever but to glance at the headlines, relieve the boredom for a minute or two. The lead story was another hotel fire, this one in Las Vegas and a disastrous one, seven people dead of smoke inhalation and more than twenty others in the hospital. I leafed casually through the top national and international stories, and still my politico hadn't come back. I glanced down the dining room and saw a crowd around the appetizer buffet and figured he'd be back soon enough and flipped the paper to page six. If Gordo hadn't chosen the same moment to refill his plate that several other parties of diners had chosen, I'd never have seen the item at the bottom of that page.

DAUGHTER OF MIDWEST SUPERMARKET CZAR DIES IN FALL

New York—The body of Ann Haskell, 32, daughter of the recently deceased Bradford Haskell, who was the founder of the nationally famous Haskell's supermarket chain, was discovered by police shortly before nine this morning in her Manhattan apartment. According to a spokesperson for the local precinct station, evidence indicated that after drinking to excess last night, Ms. Haskell had slipped on a throw rug and fallen against the brick facing of the imitation fireplace in her living room, causing a fracture of the skull.

I felt as if a lead weight had hit me in the belly. I wanted to scream. I wanted to throw my plate and glass against the wall of the restaurant and run outside and curse the sunset. All around me flowed the sea of respectable sounds, cutlery chinking, waitresses murmuring, ice tinkling in highball glasses and water goblets, the low buzz of cozy conversations. For one awful moment I wanted to kill every damn man and woman and child in the room.

Then Lardbelly squeezed himself back into the booth opposite me and started demolishing his plateful of baked stuffed clams.

It was the longest hardest evening of my life, and somehow I made myself keep in character through every gut-wrenching minute of it. I picked at the duck à l'orange and the hot bread, gulped coffee that burned my throat, bargained with the fat slug about how much of an advance I should get on my hit fee. When he dropped me at the bus stop around ten o'clock I had sixty untraceable one-hundred-dollar bills in my wallet and a black hole in the pit of my stomach that nothing in this world would fill. The New York bus came by a few minutes later, almost empty at that hour, and as the 35E hurtled north and east across the Jersey Meadowlands nightscape toward the glow of the Manhattan skyline I stared at my reflection in the dark window glass and could almost see her image there too.

The woman who was not Ann Haskell. Who I knew damn well hadn't died in any household accident. Who just a week ago this night had been with me, cuddled up against me, lying in my arms. The only woman in the world that I sort of loved.

TWO

Many people are more afraid of being known than they are of death. When they feel another person coming too close, penetrating their private space, they withdraw into a shell. When someone is threatening to know me too well, my tactic is simply to shift into another identity. This approach has worked for me consistently almost since the day I became an adult.

Only two people have ever known me.

From the notebooks of Milo Turner

The first time I saw her, she was a child and I was just out of my teens. Even then I was in the life, but still an amateur, and frankly, I tended to behave like an idiot in tight moments. The word went out from Phoenix and crossed the Southwest on phone lines that even in those pioneer days of tapping technology were checked thrice daily for bugs: Fred Schuyler, the King Fox, the supreme wizard of confidence artistry, was in the market for a young associate. I invested in a bus ticket from L.A. and he met me in person at the Phoenix Greyhound terminal and drove me in a tail-finned green Pontiac to a sprawling rancho that he'd rented on the edge of the city.

He was my spiritual father, my mentor, my rabbi. Whatever I know about the art of separating undesirables from their money stems from my time with Fred. He was at the top of his form in those last somnolent years of the Eisenhower administration, tall, white-haired, powerful of body, strong yet soft of voice, infinitely patient in instruction. We spent hours soaking up sun beside the pool next to the long low ranch house, while first we got to know each other and then we got to like each other and finally we began conspiring.

And all the time we were refining Fred's plot, a little girl splashed merrily back and forth across the pool, a blond child about seven or eight years old, her body lean and sun-toasted and her laughter bright over the dark blue water. "Found her when she was an infant," Fred told me over whisky sours late one afternoon in the ranch house den. "It was one of those damn December snowstorms and I was the only passenger on the midnight bus from Minneapolis to Grand Forks, North Dakota. I happened to go to the back of the bus to use the john and saw this bundle on a seat in the rear and turned it over to see what it was. Thought maybe it was something worth a little money that a passenger had left behind. And, by damn, it was the most valuable thing I've ever found in my life. Her mother must have fed her just before abandoning her, and that couldn't have been too long before I found her, because she stayed quiet as a mouse all through that long bus ride. The driver never knew he had an extra passenger. When I got off the bus in Grand Forks around sunrise, I took her with me. She's been mine ever since."

"You give her a name?" I asked. In my callow youth I favored a clipped, phony–hard-boiled manner of speech.

"Daughter," he said. "I'd die for that kid. In fact, she's why I'm putting together this operation now. It's my last hurrah, boy. I'm retiring from the life once it's over."

As in a blaze of insight I understood what I was doing

there in Phoenix. I was in training not just as Fred's young assistant on the big scam but as his heir.

The King Fox took infinite pains on that caper. We stayed on the ranch twenty-one days, just Fred and the child and I plus the Mexican couple that took care of the place, until I was letter perfect in my part and knew every piece of the operation as well as I knew the contours of my own face. Can anyone understand what those glorious three weeks meant to me? The excitement of being near that man, of actually working side by side with him! Imagine how a fledgling moviemaker would react to an invitation to collaborate with Orson Welles, or how the greenest second looie out of West Point would feel about a chance to discuss grand strategy with the ghost of Douglas MacArthur, and you will have a fraction of an inkling of my own awe and delight.

Our scam made its mark in history. In the years since we pulled it off, three books, a folk song, and a TV movie have been devoted to the caper. When it was over and we had enriched ourselves by just short of four million dollars, Fred went his way, out of the life and into what is laughingly called the real world, and I went mine, out of the real world and into what is laughingly called the life. I never saw that dear old man again.

Seventeen years, two or three hundred scams, and dozens of identities later, I was on a missionary visit to central Kansas under the name of the Reverend Doctor Callixtus Huckaby. My target was the governing board of a consortium of sanctimonious swindlers known as the Central States Christian Education Council, and my game was to make them underwrite a new agricultural college, to be run strictly on Fundamentalist Bible principles. The institution, of course, existed only in my nimble imagination. As part of the buildup I arranged to be interviewed on a local radio talk show. The station was owned by the CSCEC and I naturally expected that whoever was going to conduct the interview would be a dried-out prune of one sex or the other.

So much for my gift of prophecy. She turned out to be a tall lithe blonde named Nanci Newell, with a perky mobile face that failed to hide her boredom with our pious talk, and inside a modest ankle-length dress what seemed to be a smashing body. As we chatted earnestly about the need to return agricultural education to its Biblical roots, I forced myself to hold back the one question I had for her: Lady, why is a magnificent creature like yourself running a nothing talk show on a central Kansas radio station owned by a gaggle of fire-and-brimstone morons? I fought to keep any hint of the question from my face, lest it blow my pious cover into the next state.

Five days later, with a certified check for sixty-eight thousand dollars tucked away in my wallet, I boarded a bus for Topeka, where I caught a flight to Kansas City, where I turned the check into cash and ditched the Huckaby persona. Then I flew to Chicago as a commodities trader named Ralph Kahn, deposited half the take in an account I maintain as Parker W. Norton in a bank on the Loop, took another flight to Philadelphia as Daniel J. Cassidy, insurance actuary, and topped off my travels with a jaunt on the Pennsy Metroliner to New York, where I enjoy periodic sabbaticals as George Boyd. I was still there four months later.

Luxury condo living. Gourmet meals daily. Posh exercise club to keep the frame supple. The best of the world's cinema in cozy little uptown theaters. Leisurely additions to my notebooks. Literature, drama, ballet, opera, symphony, museums. Love play with elegant women on the long low bed, WNCN's chamber music concert barely audible on the night-table clock radio. It was early October when I decided that the exchequer was dwindling and it was time to create a new scam.

When I must conjure up a plot from nothing, I take long walks, which serve both to tone the bod and clear the mind. That cool autumn evening I strolled east on Central Park South, past the Essex House and the St. Moritz and the Park Lane, over to Madison and then north. Breeze heavy with promise of night rain, streetlight reflections glistening like little moons in the puddles from the last shower, long empty vista of office towers stretching uptown, a few owl cabs cruising.

And suddenly a tall cool blonde in an off-white trench coat came gliding out of the doorway of a steel and glass advertising hive and linked her arm in mine as if she'd known me all my life.

"Hello again, Milo Turner," she said, and smiled gravely at me.

To say that my stomach flip-flopped like pizza dough in the picture window of a trattoria would be the understatement of the century. Until she had spoken I would have staked my retirement accounts that no living female could tie me to what I still count as my true and original identity. For a split second I wanted to knock her into the wet street and run.

Then I looked at her more carefully; saw through the seductive trappings to what, the last time we'd met, had been the prim little cookie beneath. Nanci Newell, my corn-fed Kansas Fundamentalist lady radio talk show hostess! Had she kicked the Good Book into the gutter and blossomed forth as a lady of the New York night? What were my chances of convincing her that I really was the Reverend Doctor Callixtus Huckaby, hunting funds for my Jesus ag school along Mad. Avenue?

I put on my face the most bewildered look in my repertory and lobbed the ball back into her court. "My

11

dear lady," I said, "I regret to tell you that I don't know you and I don't think you know me."

She gave me a sweet and superior little grin. "I know you better than you realize, and this is the third walk you've taken this week when I've been behind you. Oh, don't worry, I'm no threat. We're in the same profession." She steered me deftly across Madison and east along one of the high Sixties.

"I didn't catch on to who you were until you took off with the sixty-eight thousand," she went on. "Here's a nice *intime* little bar, darling, and you may buy me a liqueur. You screwed my own game royally, you know. The governing board got so cautious after you stung them that there was no way I could take them for a penny, so I cut my losses and came back east. Chocolat Suisse," she ordered as a mess-jacketed waiter hovered over our red plush banquette.

I opted for Johnnie Red on the rocks. As I sipped the golden elixir and felt the stomach butterflies vanishing, I began to savor the lady's combination of winsome openness and devious indirection. Beneath the trench coat she wore a blue and white pantsuit that looked patriotic as God Bless America against the bright red cushions.

"You still don't remember, do you?" she said, her smile gay and mocking now. "I'll give you a hint. A ranch outside Phoenix, oh, sixteen or seventeen years ago. A big lovely pool and a little girl who sort of lived in it while you and Fred sat at a Paris-sidewalk-café kind of table and hatched some incredible scheme or other."

"Oh, my sweet God," I said softly. "You're the blond kid that swam like a fish. No wonder I didn't recognize you!" I slid over next to her on the banquette, reached for her hand, looked into startlingly deep blue eyes, dark as the water in that pool. "And you mean to say I still look enough like that twenty-year-old boy that you remembered me after I blew Kansas?"

"You've got a few more wrinkles and not quite as much hair, but by and large you've aged beautifully," she said. "I noticed you coming out of the Loew's Summit last Thursday and followed you back to Central Park South, and I've been trying to find an unobtrusive way of picking you up ever since."

"Fred's little daughter," I said under my breath, and groped for my Scotch glass and lifted it in toast to our reunion, and she raised the tiny glass that held her chocolate liqueur and tinked it against mine. And then we began to talk, and kept at it, looking into each other's eyes like recent lovers, until the bar was about to close.

"So he raised you on his own till you were ready for high school?"

"Right. And then he paid my tuition all the way through college, and threw in some fantastic summer vacations too. Europe, Acapulco, the Greek Islands . . . " She took another sip of liqueur. Tiny bits of solid chocolate stuck to the bottom of her glass. "But as I got into my early twenties he, well, seemed to withdraw from me. Didn't want me to have much to do with him. He said someday I'd fall for some fabulously rich and handsome man, and then there might be a check on his background and it would come out who I was and who he had been, and the romance would go sour."

"Did it happen that way?"

"Never came close." There was an oh-but-if-only undertone as she said it. "I took off on my own when I was twenty-one. I wanted to live the way Fred had lived when he was young. He thought I'd gone haywire. We sort of drifted out of touch, and then last January he had a coronary and just fell over outside Grand Central Station and died. No pain, thank heaven."

"I was in South America then. Didn't hear about it

till I came back a few months later. To Fred." I lifted my glass and de-Scotched it. "To the greatest." My eyes were misting a trifle, and I thought it prudent to taper off with black coffee. The waiter looked relieved at the order, with its implied hint that we'd soon be vacating the joint, and broke all speed records setting down two china mugs at our table. We sipped.

"I'm afraid I lost touch with Fred, too, after he left the life," I admitted with perhaps a touch of shame. "Didn't I hear that he invested his savings in some kind of oddball supper club here in town?"

"The Matchwit Club, on Forty-eighth just off Sixth Avenue. He started it and built it up and then took in a younger partner. Max has been running the place by himself since Fred . . . "

I probed the shadows of memory for the rest of the name. "Max . . . Yes, of course, Max Gantry, isn't it? Used to be a lawyer till they disbarred him. Wait a minute, haven't I heard on the street that he also has some sort of mysterious connection with Angelo Garza's branch of the Family?"

"You look like you've just bitten into a sour lemon with a worm in it. Don't you approve of the violent side of crime?"

"My dear, I feel about muggers and rapists and dope traffickers and hit men the way Picasso must have felt about the clowns that paint pictures for motel room walls. The way a world-class surgeon would feel about the pigstickers in the Chicago slaughterhouse. Fred Schuyler had a lot to do with my feelings, and I hope his spiritual daughter doesn't feel any different."

"She doesn't. I've never met this Angelo Garza, but I know Max Gantry all too well and I have personal reasons for despising him. That's why ever since I spotted you on the street last week I've been wrestling with how to approach you for a favor. Milo, I need your help."

"Tell me," I said quietly. Not that I'm in the business of extending kindness to strangers, but thanks to Fred we were all but brother and sister.

"Fred had a lot of money put away when he retired. He didn't use anywhere near all of it to buy the club. He told me once that he kept exactly twelve accounts in banks all over the country and Mexico, each one under a different name and with about twenty-five thousand dollars in it, give or take a few thousand."

"Ah," I said. "Another one of the brotherhood who took a leaf from the book of W. C. Fields. I do it myself, you know. It's a symptom of radical insecurity or something."

"The last time I saw Fred," she said earnestly, leaning over so close I could smell the cool flowery scent of her perfume, "I think he knew he was going to die soon. He said that if anything ever happened to him he wanted all the money in those accounts to go to me."

"He gave you the passbooks, or told you where he kept them?"

"No." I heard that oh-if-only sound again under her words. "All he said was that the key to the names of the banks and the account numbers and the names he used was somewhere in his office at the club. That's the only clue he gave me."

I downed the last of my coffee with a slurp and signaled the furious waiter for refills. "If that's all he told you he couldn't have wanted you to have the money very badly."

"No, that's not true. He was—well, superstitious, I guess, the way some people are about making a will. Giving me all the information I needed would have been like admitting he was going to die."

And would have given her the power to raid those

accounts while he was still among the living, I thought cynically, but somehow I couldn't believe that she would do that, nor that Fred would have thought she could.

"And then you have to remember," she went on, "that Fred loved puzzles. I really think that's why he chose the life. Pulling impossible scams was like solving riddles no one else could solve."

I sent my mind darting back among the twenty-one days I'd spent with the old lion in the Arizona sun. "I guess I never saw that side of him," I said slowly.

"It was practically all I did see of him, after he retired and I was growing up. Riddles, word games, anagrams, rebuses—you name it and he grooved on it. When I was in school he was always bribing me to read Poe's stories and the old fair-play detective novels, but they just never turned me on. I think by giving me only that one clue about the bank accounts he was challenging me to a game of wits. But damn it, he was too clever for me!" She bit down on her lush lower lip in frustration.

"You've actually been through his office since he died?"

"Four times," she said. "It's Max's office now. I've spent four damn nights in that office and couldn't find a shred of a clue. And Max is spending a lot more money than he can possibly be making out of the club. I'm convinced he discovered the key Fred was talking about. Fred must have been careless and dropped some hint to him and Max solved the riddle. He's as big a puzzle nut as Fred ever was."

"Maybe Fred gave Max a clue deliberately, so you and he would be in a race for the money."

She ignored my suggestion. "He's probably been draining those accounts by mail withdrawals, a few thousand dollars at a time."

"Maybe he doesn't know a damn thing about the accounts, and all his side bread's coming from Garza."

Another possibility, which she deftly dropped down her memory hole. "Milo, I need your help," she said again. "I want you to search that office in the club and try to find Fred's message for me."

"Which, if you're right, Max has probably long since found and burned."

"Not if he discovered the accounts a different way from the one Fred set up for me. If that's the case, my clue may still be sitting there. If you can find it I'll give you a third of whatever we salvage from those accounts."

I blinked and transformed myself into a mathematician. An even dozen accounts with $25,000 in each. That made a $300,000 grand total. If we could save them all, one hundred thousand for the Milonic pocket; if Gantry had cleaned them all out, nothing. I have always hated speculative ventures.

"For Fred's kid I'll gamble," I said, and reached across to take her long slender fingers in mine. She moved close to me, kissed me lightly on the mouth. God, how I wanted her that moment! The waiter glared at us like a man with a grudge, and I wondered whether our prolonged tryst was keeping him from pleasure with his own lady. I made myself pull away from her embrace and tucked a princely tip under the ashtray as we left the banquette and headed for the door and the night. We walked west, back towards Madison and, if she was in the mood, a cab to my condo. I linked my arm in hers as we trod the empty street, talking in whispers so we wouldn't wake the bag people sleeping on the steam vents.

"I forgot to ask you back there, but how did you get the chance to spend four nights searching Max's office?"

That was the one question I shouldn't have asked. She froze for a second, her face pinched under a streetlight. Then she started walking again, and as we reached the corner of Madison she looked up at me almost sadly.

"Milo, I am not a roaring success as a confidence person. Honestly, I haven't scored a single real coup in the six years I've been out. Don't ask me what's wrong with me. Maybe I'm afraid of making it. Maybe I sabotage myself, I don't know. . . . Anyway, right now I'm living on Max Gantry's money."

Oh, Jesus, I said to myself. Fred's kid sleeping with Max. I slid my arm from hers as if she were some kind of Venus's-flytrap and lifted it in a savage wave to hail a cab. The few cruisers that went by our corner kept going, speeding past like bullet cars.

She planted herself square in front of me and made me look into her eyes. "God damn you, Milo, don't *do* that to me! Listen. When I was convinced Max was into my accounts I did a little investigating and found out where he goes when he wants to pick up a new woman. I started hanging out there, and he found me and I let nature take its course. This was two months ago, pretty soon after I got back from that Kansas fiasco. Anyway, he's supporting me now. I'm living in a real nice apartment over on First Avenue. Sometimes he stays there, sometimes I go to his condo."

"Well, isn't that cozy! I suppose I'm expected to bless you with a benevolent smile."

"Stop it, you idiot! You're not the Reverend Doctor Callixtus Huckaby anymore. I did what I had to do and thanked my lucky stars Max had never met me while Fred was alive. About a week after I began going with him I was able to sneak wax impressions of his keys to the club. I had duplicates made, and that's how I got in and spent four nights searching."

"How did you know which nights he wouldn't want you?"

"Use the brains you were born with! Max doesn't believe in monogamy. I arranged for him to pick up another woman the same place I let him find me. All right?" She fumbled in her white leather purse and detached four keys from a weighted ring. "Here. Front door, back door opening on an alley, door onto the inner corridor, door to Max's office. They're yours for the duration. Do you have any more of your clever little questions?"

"Just one," I said. "Let's suppose we luck out—find the bank names, the account numbers, the phony customer names. Without passbooks and identification in each of those names, how the hell do we get the banks to turn the money over to us?"

She licked at her lips with a delectable pink tongue that was still coated slightly with chocolate from the liqueur. "I'm not such a flop in the life that I don't know who's the best document forger around," she said. "He's on Minetta Street, right?" She swung her own arm in signal for a passing cab, which braked like a screaming banshee and pulled over to the curb for us.

And dropped her off at her place on First Avenue before taking me back to Central Park South, where I spent what was left of the night in lordly solitude.

THREE

*Only when the definitive history of the confidence pro-
fession is written will Schultz's Human Supermarket be
credited as it deserves. If I still walk the earth when that
book appears, perhaps then I'll learn who owned the
disembodied voice that knew me and, if I may scramble
metaphors, watched over me as God was once said to
know and watch over His people.*

And where he got that awful Dublin brogue.

From the notebooks of Milo Turner

First step in the battle plan, since George Boyd was too
valuable a property to risk, was a new identity. I paid a
visit to Minetta Street and came away from Lafferty's
with enough paper and plastic to satisfy a casual inquirer
that I was a midlevel investment adviser named Gilbert
Dann. I rented Dann an apartment in an undistin-
guished brick building on Ninth, cabbed back to the
condo, dropped word among doormen and managers
that George Boyd was leaving for a short vacation,
packed a two-suiter, and split.

Next step was a series of meets with my client and
spiritual sister. I had no idea whether Max Gantry was a
jealous patron, so I didn't dare visit her pad on First
Avenue or invite her to mine. I chose the sites of our

get-togethers with the care of a clandestine lover: art galleries, crowded midtown eateries, modes of public transportation. Bit by bit I systematically pumped her for every detail she could remember about the Matchwit Club—its physical layout, the location of the bandstand and kitchen and rest rooms, the color and style of the waiters' attire, the number of chairs per table—until I could have built a scale model of the joint if someone supplied the materials.

George Boyd had never dined there, but I knew it by reputation, like most New Yorkers. It had the regulation soft lights, soothing music, and overpriced grub and booze, plus an attraction unique to itself—namely, its proprietor. Every night at eleven on the dot he would step up to the circular platform in the center of the main supper room, and a baby spot would bathe him in its glow and the drummer would beat out a roll to get the room's attention and the game would begin. Fred Schuyler had started the tradition and Max was carrying it on. Each night he'd tease the audience with a riddle or puzzle, and the house would pick up the tab of the lucky customer, if there was one, who could match wits with the management and win.

It was on the Staten Island Ferry, with the two of us bundled in all-weather coats and hunched over on one of the bone-hard benches on the upper deck and the wind blowing the fragrance of her hair into my face, that we went over the layout for the last time.

"Okay, here's the main room." I built a rectangle with my hands as the ferry glided past Miss Liberty. "Street door here, short corridor from the door to the main room entranceway. The wall at the far end of the main room has a door built in that you can't see unless you're looking for it. Another short corridor opens off that door. Two rooms along each side. Private john and storage area on the left, secretary's office and what used to be Max's office on the right. None of those are locked at night, just the big office at the end of the corridor, the one Max took over when Fred died."

"Perfect!" she said. "I'll bet you could find your way around the place in a total blackout."

"Now, you're absolutely certain Fred told you that the key to the bank information was *in his office*? Not just somewhere in the office area behind that door you can hardly see?"

"How many times do I have to tell you? I'd bet five years of my life on it."

"My darling," I reproved her gently, "the life you're betting may be mine." The ferry crashed and creaked against the fortress of wooden pilings as it bulled its way into the Battery pier, and I squeezed her hand as we stood up and took our leave by separate exits.

With that much of my homework done, it was time to check in with the Jock.

No one knows where he came from and no one has seen his face or bod, but the best and brightest in the life literally could not function without him. It has been conservatively estimated that without Jock Schultz and his people-emporium half the major scams of the past quarter century could not have been pulled off. If you were wired into his network and needed any imaginable human resource, Jock would find it for you—generally in a few hours or less—and call you back. No one knew how he did it. Some of my colleagues think he has a bank of computers at his fingertips like the nerve center of the CIA. A few paranoids have suggested that he *is* CIA and we his unwitting pawns in all sorts of covert operations we know nothing about. A sci-fi buff or two have hazarded the guess that he is an ET from a far galaxy who learned our language from the soundtracks of old Barry Fitzgerald movies. About all these speculations I remain agnostic. For me the essence of the Jock is that he is there. Always and definitively present.

I found a working pay phone inside the ferry terminal, punched the 1-800 number that he was using that season, jotted down the second 1-800 number the recording machine dictated to me, rearranged its digits in the order of six-four-two-seven-five-three-one, punched the new number that resulted, and heard his unmistakable stage-Irish voice at the other end. "Milo," I said. I gave him my Ninth Street name and number and asked him to call that evening with anything he could give me on the life and world of Max Gantry. We exchanged appropriate pleasantries, and I hung up and tore the scrap of paper with his disguised number on it into confetti and scattered the scraps in the gutter outside the terminal.

The phone bell jerked me awake on the couch just as Carson was launching his monologue that night. I blanked out the set and stumbled over to the phone and caught it in the middle of the seventh ring.

"Did I wake ye, Milo me buck?"

"Perish the thought, Jocko." I yawned. "What do you have?"

"Max Gantry," he began, "formerly Max Gantry, Esquire. He was an ornament of the California Bar for several years, specializing in wills, trusts, and estate planning. Then he drafted a will for a certain movie producer, which named none other than Max Gantry, Esquire as, *a,* executor of the estate, *b,* attorney for the estate, *c,* trustee of the trust the producer set up in his will for the widow and kiddies, and *d,* as attorney for the trust. He also put in the will something that I believe is known as an exculpatory clause, meaning that whatever he might do in any of his four capacities, he was immune from any and all liability. I need hardly tell ye that what he proceeded to do was to bleed the estate dry.

The widow screamed to the state bar association, and after a few years of legal squabbling the courts knocked all four of the man's hats off his silly head and disbarred him to boot. In time he pulled a reverse Horace Greeley and resettled in New York and became Fred Schuyler's partner in the Matchwit Club."

"I can't believe Fred would have taken in a creep like that," I said.

"Ye didn't know that grand old divil in his twilight time," Jock reminded me sadly. "He'd lost the magic, me bhoy. And ah, if it happened to Fred, ye know sure as death that someday it will happen to you. And me."

"Not anytime soon," I said, or perhaps *prayed* would be the more accurate word. "Okay, let's change the subject. What kind of security does he have at the club?" Not much, I had already reasoned, since my lady had searched the place uncaught on four separate occasions.

"Just the standard alarm system that a child could disconnect and turn on again without a trace. Ye'll have not a bit of bother with it. But ye'll need to watch for his human security, or do ye know about the Moose already?"

"He keeps a live moose? You mean like a guard dog? Jocko, if you have a nose on your face it just grew a yard."

"More dangerous than the animal this one is, me lad. He has on his payroll a bruiser who calls himself Moose Eliot. It's a phony name, I suspect, but ye'll know him soon as ye see or even hear him. His face looks to be carved out of pork fat, and he bears a faint resemblance to a bloated corpse. He has a nervous habit of whistling but he's so bloody awful at carrying a tune, half the time he couldn't tell you what he was whistling if you paid him a thousand dollars. But the man weighs over three hundred pounds, and if he got his arms around you he'd break you like a toothpick."

"Ecchh." I felt sweat trickle down my back as I real-

25

ized what I might encounter on this scam. "And this Moose hangs out at the club?"

"He spends the entire night there two or three times a week, so I'm told. Gantry picks the nights at random."

"Oh, Christ," I muttered.

"Something wrong with ye, lad?"

I had just realized that only by pure dumb luck had my lady chosen nights to search the premises that Gantry hadn't picked for the Moose to be on duty. Now if only I could be so fortunate. "Nothing," I said. "I can handle him if I have to. I hope. Look, Jock, is the supermarket open?"

"For special customers we never close. How can I serve ye?"

"Who on this island can be hired at a reasonable fee to make me up a jacket on special order?" I specified my sartorial requirements in vivid detail.

During the ensuing fifteen seconds of silence over the line I could almost hear the electronic song of computers at the other end. Then he had a name for me. "Solly," he said, and added an address and phone number. "Theatrical tailor. I believe he learned the trade in Attica."

"Thanks, Jock. I'll let you know how it goes," I promised, and wished him good night and went back to the kingdom of sleep.

The next morning I called the number to make an appointment with Mr. Solly, and on my way to lunch I visited his cramped little shop in a Fourth Avenue loft and left with him the jacket of my best midnight-blue three-piece suit and precise instructions on how he was to embellish it. Two days later he called back to tell me my order was ready. I cabbed over and picked up the jacket, encased in a brown paper wrapper to which was attached an infuriatingly hefty bill.

"Inflation." He shrugged eloquently and held out his dirt-caked palm.

FOUR

The joy and curse of my profession is the joy and curse of life in general: unpredictability. Sometimes I have worked on a scam night and day for months, and my plot has danced to its culmination as gracefully as a prima ballerina. At other times one pinpoint glitch, beyond mortal power to foresee or control, has made me junk an operation on which I had sweated blood for half a year. More than once I have walked without preparation or forethought into what looked like a magnificent opportunity and gotten my fingers scorched. Just as often I have gone in more or less on impulse and come out clutching the golden cookie jar.

There is probably a lesson in this somewhere.

From the notebooks of Milo Turner

The time had come to make my first pass at the target.

I phoned the Matchwit Club and made a nine o'clock dinner reservation for Gilbert Dann. With first the local news and then the national news and finally a sitcom furnishing the background noise, I killed the early evening garnishing myself for the occasion. Gray contact lenses hid my eye color, a neatly trimmed salt-and-pepper wig gave me a new hairline (not to mention hair), and artfully positioned chunks of theatrical rubber reshaped the contours of my phiz. At eight thirty I killed the apartment lights, flagged a cab outside the street door of my building. I paid the driver at the corner of Sixth Avenue and Forty-eighth. When the doorman flung open one of the huge double doors of the club for me I looked the perfect image of a jowly single in a three-piece midnight-blue suit, out for an evening of innocuous fun. I hoped.

My study sessions made the place as comfortably familiar as an old shoe. A short corridor took me from the front doors to the main room. Just opposite the entranceway a gorgeous black chick in a see-through gown presided over the checkroom. Inside the main chamber a maître d' in black tie ticked off Dann's name on his reservations roster and entrusted me to a waiter in a red bolero jacket, who led me most of the way across the room to a small but elegantly appointed table. Lucky Break Number One: I had a good view of the raised circular platform from which Gantry launched his riddles. I ordered a Dewar's sour on the rocks with an extra twist of orange and glanced casually around the room as I sipped. For a weeknight it was satisfactorily filled, maybe two hundred people in all, mostly parties of two or three or four, both sexes, all ages, few nonwhites except for the busboys. The after-hours chatter was a low rumble like distant thunder that I quickly tuned out. For dinner I chose Chateaubriand medium rare, with chives and bacon bits on the twice-baked potato, house dressing on the salad, lots of coffee. I savored every mouthful like a soldier on his last night of leave before the big battle. A few minutes short of eleven I beckoned the waiter and asked for my check.

All of a sudden the drummer on the bandstand was beating out a long shuddery roll. Max Gantry came out of nowhere and threaded his way between tables to the platform and bowed to the wave of applause that pounded across the dining room as he stepped into the light of the baby spot. He looked about five seven, which was shorter than I had imagined him, but with his high forehead and neat little mustache and the hooded look around the eyes as if he was keeping some heavy thoughts from the rest of the world, he projected all the suavity and savoir faire of a celluloid secret agent.

The third point of the triangle whose center was Fred Schuyler. We other two, Fred's first son and his only daughter, we knew one another and now we both knew Max, but he had no idea that he'd been sleeping with one of us for the past two months nor that he was providing dinner tonight—and, if I were very lucky and very skillful, maybe a lot more than dinner—for the other.

The applause fell to silence and Gantry stopped bowing to various corners of the room and came up to the microphone stand on the platform. "Thank you, ladies and gentlemen," he said, his voice low and penetrating like a politician's or a gigolo's, "and welcome to the Matchwit Club. I'm Max Gantry, your host. My story tonight was one of the favorites of—of my dear friend and partner Fred Schuyler, the founder of this club, who died last January." His voice broke for a split second. "The closest thing to a father I've ever known. . . . I suppose you might call it an It Couldn't Have Happened story. If anyone here tonight can explain how it did happen—well, you know the rule. Whatever you and your party have eaten and drunk tonight is on the house. Are you ready?"

"Hit us, Maxie!" roared a liquor-sodden baritone across the room.

"One fine afternoon in Central City, U.S.A., three gentlemen stepped into the lobby of the Acme Hotel and requested a room for the night. 'We have a very nice room on the thirteenth floor,' the clerk said. 'How much will it be?' the men asked. 'Thirty dollars,' the clerk told them. 'Payable now,' he added when he saw that none of the three was carrying luggage. Each of the men took a ten-dollar bill from his wallet and handed it to the clerk.

Then the three guests went upstairs in the elevator to room thirteen thirteen, where they'd been assigned.

"About an hour later the clerk happened to glance at the list of the hotel's room prices and realized that he'd overcharged the three men. The correct rate for room thirteen thirteen was not thirty but only twenty-five dollars. The clerk took five singles out of his cash drawer, rang for a bellboy, and instructed the boy to give the money to the three gentlemen in thirteen thirteen.

"The bellboy happened to be alone going up in the elevator. Suddenly he had a bright but rather dishonest idea. He took two of the five singles while the cage was going up and stuffed them in his shoe. When he got off the elevator and knocked on the door of thirteen thirteen, he told the three men that the correct room rate was twenty-seven dollars, not the thirty they'd paid—in other words, that the clerk had overcharged them three dollars. Then he handed one dollar bill to each of the three and bowed politely and went back downstairs, transferring the bills he'd stolen from his shoe to his wallet in the elevator.

"Now, ladies and gentlemen, do all of you understand what happened that day at the Acme Hotel?"

A chorus of assent exploded from the audience.

"Well," he said with an omniscient smirk in his voice, "let's see if you do. Now, each of the three men originally paid the clerk ten dollars. Right?"

"Right!" a few brave voices echoed. They were the Matchwit Club veterans, I guessed.

"And each of them got one dollar back. Right?"

"Right!" Louder this time. The first-timers were entering into the spirit of the game.

"So the net result was that they were each paying nine dollars for the room. Right?"

Either the logic or the math of the statement seemed to elude some of the choristers, for the "Right!" that echoed back this time was wimpy compared with the earlier roar.

"And nine times three is twenty-seven," Gantry continued smoothly, "which is the number of dollars the men wound up paying for the room. Right?"

The only response was silence: the audience was losing its nerve. I'd allowed myself only the one Scotch sour more than two hours ago, but I couldn't figure out where Max's tale was going any better than the customers who had guzzled far more grain than I.

At that moment I experienced what my Zen Buddhist friends call a *satori,* an overpowering intuition of what it's all about. Mine, unfortunately, was just a minisatori, but it opened up for me one of the secrets of the Matchwit Club. People tend to stuff themselves when they dine at all-you-can-eat buffets, and one of the reasons they overeat at those places is that they have a weird notion that beyond a certain point they are getting something for nothing. This club was a sort of psychological buffet: people tended to drink too much precisely because they hoped to beat Max in the game and see the evening's bill torn up. But the overindulgence fuddled the customers' wits, so that their chances of solving the puzzle hovered around the zero mark! I filed away the strategy in my gray cells for possible future use in a scam of my own.

"And twenty-seven dollars," Max went on, "plus the two the bellboy stuffed in his shoe, makes twenty-nine. Right?"

A few none too confident voices threw back "Right!" at him.

"So. Now, which of you ladies or gentlemen cares to tell me *what happened to the thirtieth dollar?*" Gantry spread his manicured hands palm out as if to show that the dollar wasn't on him.

First there was half a minute of stunned silence. Then

a buzz of whispers erupted all over the room as diners put their heads together and muttered various theories to each other. Plates of outrageously priced food grew cold, drinks stood untouched, coffee went unsipped. I was in the presence of a master, all right. Gantry had those two hundred suckers under his control as if he'd hypnotized them.

A tall fortyish woman in a green off-the-shoulder gown lurched to her feet, mounted her chair clumsily with help from the two men at her table, cupped her hands around her mouth. "The, ah, the billboy dropped the bell on the elevator floor!" she shouted at the platform.

Gantry bowed his head slightly like a mourner at graveside. "I'm sorry, madam, that is not correct." The woman fell off the chair and dejectedly resumed her seat.

An old man with thinning white hair stood to make his try. "One of the three men only paid the clerk nine bucks to begin with," he croaked.

"No, sir. You'll recall I distinctly said that each of them paid with a ten-dollar bill."

A few more hands went up hesitantly in the audience and a little voice in my head told me, *Now, man.* Willing myself to be invisible I rose and sauntered in the direction of the men's room, passed through the swing door into the white-tiled dazzlement. Lucky Break Number Two: it was empty. The run on the john would come when the game was over.

I locked myself into a cubicle, doffed my wig, and secured it with rubber bands against my calf. The contact lenses went into their case in my hip pocket, the cheek rubber down the toilet. I tore off my dark four-in-hand and replaced it with a red bow tie. Then, last step in the transformation, I turned the jacket of my midnight-blue suit inside out, and presto! thanks to Solly the Wizard Tailor, I held in my hand a garment of fire-engine red. Following the old pirate's directions and the chalk marks he'd made on the material, I used a handful of safety pins from my pocket to tuck the vents up the back so that the jacket fell only to my waist. Elapsed time from the moment I'd walked into the john was forty-seven seconds. I was now indistinguishable in dim light, or so I fondly hoped, from the two-dozen-odd waiters who served the tables of the Matchwit Club.

The next few minutes were tricky. The hired help had their own sanitary facilities off the kitchen. If I were caught in that outfit in the paying customers' john, there went the ball game. I tiptoed to the exit door of the men's room and eased it open just enough of a crack so that I could see a bald fatty on his feet trying to expound on his solution and Max diplomatically striving to cut the guy off and give someone else a chance. I slid out of the john quick as a red rabbit and drifted over to the bar, where I palmed a pad of service checks and picked up a drink tray from a handy stack. Then I approached the far corner of the bar area, where the mixologist was working his magic.

"Two Grand Marnier," I ordered.

Loud groans from the customers in the dining area told me that Max was bringing the game to a halt. I turned and threaded my way along the main room's far wall, drink tray balanced neatly on one palm. The crowd gave Gantry a loud if grudging hand as he swept off the platform toward the entranceway and out of the club—his custom every evening, my lady had assured me, so that he wouldn't have to contend with any midnight quarterbacks who wanted to challenge the fairness of the latest riddle. The waiters spread out across the room to take the thirsty multitude's postgame drink orders.

With a servingman's deliberate speed I edged close to the unobtrusive door in the wall that led to the office area and Max's sanctum. Painted the same color as the wall, no outside knob, the thin line around its edges almost invisible in the half light. It was about as well camouflaged as a door in a public area could be.

That was when the temptation smacked me between the eyes like a two-by-four.

All of a sudden that door was irresistible. It was as if I'd just come home to find the world's most beautiful woman performing a naked love dance for me on my living room rug. My brain went haywire, my sense of self-preservation conked out, and my only goal this side of the grave was to walk through that door—and not anytime later, but right this minute, while the club was still a-hop with life.

The original plan, the one my rational self had devised, was so much simpler and safer. Play waiter till the joint shut down at midnight, duck behind the bar until the last of the hired help had left, then enjoy the run of the place till six A.M., when the cleaning crew would check in. But that siren voice in my skull kept singing *Don't wait, man, do it now*! Max was gone for the night, the office area was bound to be deserted at this hour and had more hidey-holes than the public part of the club. And I'd gain some extra hunting time to boot.

The voice convinced me.

I made a beeline from the wall to a temporarily vacant table two rows in and deposited the liqueur glasses from my tray. When those customers returned from the rest room they would find and I hoped would enjoy the excellent Grand Marnier they hadn't ordered. I drifted over toward the spot in the wall again, reached into my hip pocket for the set of duplicate keys to the club, fingered each till I touched the tiny triangle of electrician's tape that I'd used to mark the one that fit the wall door, dug that key out, and stabbed it into the lock. No one stopped me. I slipped through, pushed the door shut behind me. The voices and click of glasses and cutlery turned to stone silence: good soundproofing. In front of me was the short carpeted corridor I knew so intimately from my homework lessons, two closed doors on either wall, another at the far end thirty feet away, midget night-light plugged into a wall socket halfway down so I wouldn't have to stumble in the dark. I tiptoed to the corridor's end, found the key to Gantry's office, used it, shut that door behind me.

The room was efficient but elegant too. Massive conference desk with a high-backed executive swivel chair tucked behind it. Deadly-looking letter opener with a Buddha handle lying across the blotter. Desktop bare of papers. Ornamental pen set, flush with the outer edge of the polished mahogany. Brace of walnut-stained file cabinets along the wall at right angles to the desk, within easy reach of whoever sat in the executive swivel. Couple of overstuffed visitor chairs, leather couch flanked by end tables. Fat-bellied lamp on occasional table against a side wall. Lucky Break Number Three: it was lit. I looked down and saw it was attached to a timer that would turn the light off and on periodically so as to fool potential burglars. The dial told me that the lamp was set to go out at 1:15.

I didn't touch anything, just stood in the center of the room trying to absorb its feel. I had no idea what I was looking for and—considering that the last hunter had wasted four nights here—little hope of finding it. Whatever clue Fred had left for her had most likely been deep-sixed by Max Gantry months ago.

I ran my eyes along the walls. One window, behind the desk, shrouded in room-darkening drapes. Wires from the alarm system ran out from under the drapes and along the baseboard. I didn't dare get too near the window. The other walls were bare except for a few drab prints and an advertising calendar that was partly obscured by the shade of the fat-bellied table lamp.

So this was where Fred Schuyler had worked in his twilight years. I wondered how much Gantry had changed the decor. Somehow that calendar didn't seem at home in the muted elegance of the office furnishings. I peered behind the lampshade to study it. It was a current 1976 calendar all right: Fred had probably hung it on the wall late last year, before he'd had his coronary in January. And it was turned to October, so Max was clearly using it. The upper half featured a color photograph of a post office or a courthouse. Underneath the picture caption and just above the centerfold there was printed a black-bordered box with *Compliments of the Law Offices of Edgar A. Perry* inside it.

That was the moment of my maxisatori.

Memories meshed, forming a perfect mosaic. Her voice: "When I was in school he was always bribing me to read Poe's stories . . . but they just never turned me on." The voice of C. Auguste Dupin in Poe's "The Purloined Letter," expatiating on the best hiding place being the most open and obvious spot. The voice of a life of Poe I'd read a few years ago, reminding me that as a young man, that haunted wretch had used the pseudonym of Edgar A. Perry. The voice of a fact, later altered by the Supreme Court but still true in 1976: It is a violation of the canons of professional ethics for lawyers to advertise, so there can be no such animal as an advertising calendar from a law firm. I had learned this during a scam when I had to convince three hopelessly corrupt attorneys that I was a member of their learned profession.

Gently I lifted the calendar from the hook that it hung on, making damn sure I touched only its supporting cord and not the paper. I studied the October layout, then flipped backward and forward to compare it with the layout for other months. Nothing at all out of line. Each date figure was encased in a standard square box, the photograph above each month leaf was some public building or other.

I bent closer to the page to study the date boxes more closely. For each month, there were fine-print annotations beneath anywhere from three to seven of the date figures, indicating the importance of that date in legal history. The March eighth box read, "1841—Birth of Justice Oliver Wendell Holmes." The box for February ninth said, "1803—*Marbury v. Madison* decision handed down by Supreme Court." June seventeenth was another biggie for lawyers: "1934—*Denver First National Bank v. Theodore Donahue* decided by Colorado's high court." And likewise July thirtieth: "1907—New York Court of Appeals' historic decision in *Brooklyn Savings & Loan v. Andrews & Williams Corp.*"

And suddenly it dawned on me that here was I on a desperate search for information about some banks and here in my sticky hands was this dubious calendar that seemed to be overloaded with bank references. I flipped back to January and skimmed the date boxes. Bingo! A banking law ruling. Turned to February. Voila! Another. Likewise with March and April. Another minute and I'd confirmed my suspicion. Every month in the year included the anniversary of one and only one decision on the law of financial institutions. Twelve in all. The exact number of accounts I was hunting for.

Believe that could be coincidence, friend, and for a measly million bucks I'll sell you the skull of the ass on which Jesus rode into Jerusalem.

I tore a ballpoint pen from my bolero jacket's breast pocket, patted myself frantically for scratch paper. Nothing. Wait, damn it, the pad of service checks I'd filched from the bar! I ripped it out of my trouser pocket and began scrawling down every date to which was attributed a great legal event, bank-related or not. With up to seven annotated dates per month, the process consumed a few minutes and the backs of most of my bar checks.

I was finishing September when I heard a noise that turned my backbone into a stalactite.

It was a noise that a then wildly popular TV sitcom called *All in the Family* had converted from a commonplace into what I might punningly call a running joke.

The flushing of a toilet.

In that private john not twenty feet down the corridor from where I stood like a victim of Medusa.

Then came a sound that scared me twice as much as the toilet. It was whistling. Loud, penetrating, and wildly off key. It might have been a tune from a Broadway musical or the Battle on the Ice theme from Prokofiev's *Alexander Nevsky.*

Of all the lousy breaks! My lady haunts these rooms four nights unscathed, and I run into one of Moose Eliot's random night watches ten minutes after I stroll in. Why the hell did he have to begin his tour of guard duty before the club closed down? What would I do if he strolled down the inner corridor to this office?

Then the sound of his whistling was smothered by the roar of a hand-drying machine, and the voice in my head screamed *Now, man! The hell with the rest of the year!* With thirty seconds max at my disposal I stuffed the bar checks into a pocket, hung the calendar back on its wall hook, ran to and opened the door—God, no more hand-dryer blasting!—shut it behind me, flew up thirty feet of corridor, opened the door in the main room wall, and got it closed at literally the split second that I heard the door of the private john snicking open behind me. I thanked heaven that the Moose believed in washing his hands thoroughly after a crap.

In the dining room I assumed my waiter walk again, *Slow down man,* sweating like a broiling pig beneath the red jacket. It took me close to five minutes to meander nonchalantly across the room, past parties of customers settling their bills, and through the arched entranceway and past the checking facility from which the stunning black chick was momentarily absent. The outer corridor was empty. In two blinks I had unfastened the safety pins and reversed my jacket from the red back to the midnight-blue side and smoothed out the folds and opened one of the massive double doors and walked calmly out past the portalkeeper and into the cool dark delicious security of a midtown New York street in the hour before midnight.

FIVE

Several years ago, when the exigencies of a scam required me to manage a porno bookstore in Boston, I killed the boring workdays actually reading a few dozen specimens of that genre. The conclusion I reached matched that of certain social critics, namely that the essence of pornography is its creation of an absurdly hospitable world. Every time the hero blinks, there lies another beauty naked and panting for him, and he sends each of them plus himself into transports of orgasm time and time again. Such is the escapist fantasy of pornography. We who inhabit the real world know that life is just not that hospitable.

Not sexually, anyway.

From the notebooks of Milo Turner

I walked east on Forty-eighth and south on Lex a few blocks, then flagged a cab that was unloading at a corner and said, "Port Authority." My heart was still pounding like Gene Krupa on drums when I shoved bills through the slot in the cab's security partition and strolled into the terminal and rode the escalator down to the subway level and caught a local that spat me out a few blocks from Ninth Street. *Walk slow, dummy,* the voice kept telling me. It took supreme control not to start yipping for joy and breaking into a wild gleeful run.

I passed a bar and poked my snoot in the doorway, saw a pay phone within reach and fed a dime into the slot and tapped out the digits of her number. Two rings, three, then I heard her sleep-heavy voice and only at the last moment remembered the code we'd prearranged in case either of us had a guest when the other called. "Jerry there?" I asked.

"Dunno any Jerry. You gotta wrong number," she mumbled furiously, and hung up. Suddenly cold sweat was pouring down my sides again. At this hour her only possible visitor would be Max Gantry, and if he stayed the night I'd have to possess my soul in patience and wait for her to call me when she could. Perversely I almost wished him joy, because if the notes I'd taken in the Matchwit Club office meant what I thought they did, it would be the last night he'd ever spend in her bed.

I let myself into my apartment, secured all three of the police locks behind me, tossed my clothes into a heap on the floor, stood under roaring hot shower spray till I was the color of steak tartare and free of adrenaline rush. Then I crawled into pajamas and bed and bunched up pillows for a neck and back rest and switched on the night-table radio to a chamber music program on WQXR and studied the notations I'd scrawled on those bar checks until every fact and figure was locked into the Milonic brain. God, if only I had some lawbooks in the apartment, I could check out some of the dates on the Perry calendar without waiting for morning! *Forget it. Stop thinking and go to sleep.*

I couldn't turn myself off. The excitement had affected my system like a gallon of black coffee, and not even the sweet strains of the Dvořák piano quintet relaxed me. Finally, somewhere around three A.M., I punched on the night-table lamp and plunked the bedside phone extension down on my chest and called the Jock.

His wee-hours voice was indistinguishable from his voice at any normal time of day, and I wondered as I had many a time before if that detached presence ever needed sleep. "Me," I announced myself. "With news." And I regurgitated for him the night's events including a full word picture of the calendar on the Matchwit Club's office wall.

He caught the clues without even a nudge from me. "Edgar A. Perry ye say?" he repeated softly. "An attorney named Edgar A. Perry touting his services on a calendar?"

"I thought you'd see it. Do you see how the code works too?"

"Case names and dates," he said. "Ah, that sly old Fred was King Fox to the last! I tip me tam-o'-shanter to his ghost."

"It must be. The clue to each account number is the dates that important legal happenings are credited to in a given month. The hell with whether the dates are historically correct. Let's suppose that April fourth, ninth, seventeenth, eighteenth, twenty-third, and twenty-ninth are marked as great days in the law." Not wishing to subject the Jock to temptation, I was careful to avoid the dates that were actually annotated on the Perry calendar. "That means that one of the account numbers we want is four nine seven eight three nine. I'm assuming that the first digit of any two-digit date is irrelevant because Fred had no control over them beyond being able to choose among one, two, or three."

"A reasonable hypothesis so far," Jock commented sagely. "But now how do ye find the name of the bank and the name Fred used to set up the account?"

"As if you didn't know," I said. "Those names are on the calendar, too, if you know how to read it. Each of the twelve months has one and only one reference to a decision that includes both the name of a bank and the name of a human being. Here's what it says under June seventeenth, for example: Nineteen fourteen—*Topeka National Bank versus Ernest Cox* decided by Kansas Supreme Court.'" Another minor alteration of the calendar data purely for security's sake. "I'm going to a law library in the morning to make sure, but I'd lay money this minute that every one of these banking law decisions is a fake. Those twelve case names were put there to give the bank's name and the depositor's name that Fred used. Twelve names, twelve account numbers—just like he told his kid."

"I wouldn't bet against ye," the Jock said. "It's proud I am of how ye pulled it off, and proud Fred would be too that he chose ye."

"It was like an explosion in my head that blew everything into place instead of the opposite," I told him with, I fear, a patch of awe still in my voice, as if I'd been participant in a miracle. "The calendar, the story about the three men in the hotel—suddenly everything fit, everything belonged! Remember, Gantry even said on the platform that that riddle was one of Fred's favorites."

"Well, naturally I saw the answer to the riddle meself as soon as ye recounted it," the Jock said with a modest cough, "but perhaps ye'd enjoy telling me yer own solution."

"There is no thirtieth dollar," I said. "It's false mathematics and the way the story is told that make it seem as if there is. Change the manner of telling it just a bit and all the thirty bucks are accounted for. The proper room rate is twenty-five, the bellhop returned three, which makes twenty-eight, and kept two, which makes thirty."

"And no one else of that mob in the club even came close! Tell me, boyo, are you and I superior beings or is everyone else on the planet a potatohead?"

"Those people aren't in the business of giving apparent reality to what doesn't exist," I pointed out. "Like an extra dollar bill, or a bunch of banking law decisions." Or an extra red-jacketed waiter, I might have added, or a Jesus-based agricultural college. "Fred was and I am.

Max Gantry has never been in that corner of the life, which explains why he never noticed the calendar clue." And it was no wonder that my lady, with her rueful admission that she was a flop as a confidence person, hadn't made the connection either.

"Well," the Jock said, "congratulations again, and godspeed cleaning out the accounts, provided Mr. Gantry has left anything in them for ye. Give an old fool's best to Fred's daughter, and—ah, tell her to call me someday."

I wished him goodnight and darkened the room and killed the radio, and with the Jockian benediction soothing me I drifted into sleep.

Until the phone went off like shotgun blasts in my ears.

I screamed *"Whazzat?"* half awake, and saw dawn streaks at the window and heard the roar of garbage trucks on Ninth and read 6:52 on the digital alarm and cursed and yanked up the handset in a grip that would have strangled the phone if it had been a living thing. "Joe's Fish Market and Massage Parlor," I roared. "Whattahellyawan?"

"Chocolate Suisse." It was her voice, still sounding exhausted. "Sorry I couldn't call sooner, dear, but I just kissed Max good-bye ten minutes ago. I'm going to crawl back under the covers and sleep till supper. . . . What's the word?"

"Victory," I told her calmly. "I think. Another few hours and I should know for sure. Look, before you conk out again, pack a suitcase and get ready for a quick move either across town or across the country. Then you can sleep all you want, unless I call with instructions. Clear?"

"That's all I get told?" she complained. "I thought you were an enlightened progressive about equality of the sexes!"

"I'm also an extreme paranoid about phones," I lied. "Sleep well, darling."

My first stop that morning was a doughnut joint a block from the apartment, where I fueled myself with a glazed cruller and coffee. Then I cabbed north to Forty-second and walked east to Fifth and mounted the grand staircase between the lions of the New York Public Library. The next few hours of my life were spent in the high-ceilinged room where they kept the law collection. I had picked up a smattering of legal research technique during some scams where I'd passed myself off as an attorney, and found that I could check out the information on the Perry calendar without prodigious effort.

Confirmation all the way. Some of the listed dates were correct and some weren't—*Marbury v. Madison* for example had been handed down not on the ninth of February as the calendar claimed but on the twenty-fourth—but the alphabetical indices to the Decennial Digests of every reported judicial decisions in the United States listed not a solitary one of the banking law decisions on the calendar. I was out of the library in ample time for lunch at a McAnn's, the bar-and-grill chain that serves the tastiest beef-in-a-basket in New York.

Replete with bacon cheeseburger, french fried potatoes, french fried onions, and a stein of dark Bavarian, I stopped at a pay phone on the corner, tapped out Directory Assistance, and asked for the number of the Wall Street branch of Bankers Trust. Half a minute later I was requesting that the receptionist voice on the other end connect me with Mr. Martin Siegel. "That line is busy will you hold please?" So he still worked there. I hung up and waved for a taxi.

In the shadow of our mightiest financial institutions I turned in at the corner of Wall and Nassau and stepped over to an authoritative-looking woman seated behind a gleaming desk and asked for Mr. Siegel.

"Your name, please?" she barked.

"Arthur Lattman."

That was one of my dearest identities, for as I had created him and lived the role at odd moments, Arthur Lattman was a knight of the big town, a hero for our time, or in plain English, a private eye, op, dick, peeper, shamus, whatever. Three years ago I had rented a midtown office under that name as part of an elaborate scam and had been visited out of the blue and at the most awkward possible moment by a real live client, a tall, thin, intense-looking young banker wearing wire-rimmed specs that made him look like an assistant professor of something dreary. His name was Martin J. Siegel, his sexual preference was one that our stodgier banks frown upon, and he desperately needed to recover some photographs of himself holding hands in a bar with a Hispanic stud in a black mesh muscle shirt, which had been shot on the sly by a couple of amateurs at the art of the shakedown. Purely for the hell of it I had glommed the goods for him and then sent the paparazzi packing by the simple ploy of framing them for a recent knife murder. Young Siegel's gratitude when I handed him the glossies and negs had been pathetic.

As the authority lady shepherded me toward his cubicle I was mentally cooking an explanation, in case one were needed, of why Arthur Lattman had dematerialized for the past three years. Wasted effort. When I entered his square of private space and plunked my butt in his visitor's chair, he looked up from whatever financial report he was reading with an air of resentfulness at the interruption, but then as he saw who had wandered in he blinked like a man confronting a ghost and bounded to his feet and all but stood at attention and thrust out his hand to mine and pumped with the vigor of a politician on the stump. "My God, Mr. Lattman! God, but it's great to see you again! What are you doing here? What can I do for you?" Not only did he ask no searching questions but he was almost pitiably eager to please, as I had counted on him to be.

"I'm only back in town for a day or so," I said, as if I had told him long ago where I had relocated. "On business. I can't tell you much about the case, but I'm trying to bail out another guy who's in a mess through no fault of his own. And you can help me do it, if you will."

The pitch was carefully calculated so that he'd slit his throat before he'd refuse me, and it worked. "Anything!" he promised grandly. Then he took a breath to consider what a sweeping commitment he'd just made, and backpedaled. "That is, anything legal and within reason." He is a man destined to climb high up the banking ladder.

"I need confirmation that certain accounts exist and the current balance in each that does." I handed him a neatly recopied list of the hypothetical accounts as I'd reconstructed them from the January through September sheets of the Perry calendar. "Can you run these through the telex for me?"

He rubbed his chin fiercely and peered around the cubicle as if fearful of an eavesdropping superior, then swung his specs back to me. "Is it really important?" he asked in a plotter's whisper.

"Vital," I assured him.

"Will tomorrow do?"

"Now." I pushed him, freighted the word with the silent reminder *You owe me,* because I couldn't afford to wait an extra minute.

"It will take half an hour or so. Excuse me, please." He slipped the data sheet into a manila folder with the bank's name embossed on the front, rose, stretched, donned the jacket of his gray cashmere suit, and vanished through the doorless doorway. I crossed my ankles and closed my eyes and treated myself to a catnap while the bank machinery hummed for me.

This was the moment of truth. If the nine accounts existed and contained money, I would know that I'd cracked the code and that Gantry hadn't bled the system dry. If they didn't exist now, it might mean that I'd screwed up the code or it might mean that Gantry had closed them out, and either way I'd be, as a property lawyer might put it, up the creek with no riparian rights.

Banks have a strict policy of not telling you a word about a particular account unless you can prove the account belongs to you. Trying to get that kind of information over the phone or through any routine channel is a waste of time. But you can do it if you happen to know a bank loan officer who is in to you for a favor. All loan officers have access to the credit-checking network that comes into play whenever someone applies for a bank loan. Any bank in the country will honor another bank's request for the status of an account if the query is transmitted over the telex as a simple credit check. It's a system that makes me feel naked and vulnerable and has permanently inhibited me from borrowing money. From a bank, I prefer to steal.

The thirty minutes Siegel had mentioned went by, and another twenty in their wake, and I had resorted to the desperate step of leafing through the banking journals stacked on a credenza behind his desk by the time he finally slipped back into the cubicle and into his brown leather chair.

"Sorry it took so long," he said.

"No problem," I said, stoically hiding my excitement like the Spartan kid with the fox under his cloak. "Do— do those accounts exist?"

"You bet they do," he told me.

My heart leapt up as if I'd seen a rainbow in the sky—

as indeed I had, one with pots of gold at the end of it. "All nine of them?"

"Eight, anyway. We can't check the one with Banco Nacional de Mexico because Mexican banks aren't tied into the network. But the U.S. accounts are real all right."

"Then the Mexican one must be too," I said. "Now, ah, how much is in each of the accounts today?" I did some instant mental arithmetic. Fred had said that each one held about twenty-five thousand dollars. Multiplied by nine, that made a max of just under a quarter million. How much of that had Gantry pulled out in the nine or ten months since Fred's death? I pushed myself to the foremost two inches of the visitor's chair and braced for his answer.

"Here are the current balances." He bent closer to the work sheet I'd given him and I could see a neat figure inked in next to each listed account. "Citizens Trust Bank of Atlanta, eighty-six thousand, six hundred thirty-two dollars and seventy-nine cents. United States National Bank of Oregon, nine hundred twenty-nine thousand, eight hundred forty-four dollars and one cent. First National Bank of Denver . . ." He droned out figures that came close to blowing the top of my head off, made me want to leap onto his desktop and dance like Zorba the Greek. The skimpiest of the numbers was in the high forty thousands and the fattest approached the million mark, for a grand total—and rest assured that it was a *very* grand total—of around fifteen hundred thousand crustaceans. A mil and a half.

He handed the work sheet across to me and I sat there goggling moronically at the figures for so long that he began to give me anxious squints through his bifocals. "Mr. Lattman? You okay? Would a glass of water help?"

Then my head rebounded from the cubicle ceiling and stabilized again between my shoulders, and I realized what those hefty numbers meant. "Thanks, no." I stowed the work sheet in my wallet, lurched out of my chair, and held out my hand in a farewell shake. "Just forget you saw me."

And I stumbled out of the bank and into the cold sunlight of Wall Street, blinking like a mole and thinking like a fury. So that's the connection between Max and Angelo Garza. He cracked Fred's banking system and sold it to Garza as a laundry for Mafia money.

I flung out my arm for a cab and told the jockey to fly me to Sixth Avenue and Ninth Street.

SIX

Few of the old saws beloved of our schoolteachers are worth the breath to repeat them, but there is one that cannot be repeated too often: Knowledge is Power. The mark of the successful confidence person, indeed of the successful person in any field, is that he knows more than everyone around him. And there is a special pleasure and a special power when one is able to recite mentally, in the singsong of a child mocking another child, the magic formula of superiority: I know something you don't know.

From the notebooks of Milo Turner

As the cab crawled north I indulged in a fantasy. I saw my beautiful lady and myself winging joyously to one of the cities on my work sheet, establishing identities there, infiltrating the target bank by one brilliant ruse or another, making a Xerox copy of the signature card on a certain bulging account, cleaning out the money with a forged withdrawal slip, then flying merrily to the next city and doing it over again, until all eight of the accounts were drained. Half a mil for me and a cool million for her, on whose interest she could live comfortably for the rest of her days so that she'd never have to rent her bod again. Such was my reverie as I passed a five to the wheelman and trotted along Ninth Street. Once inside the Gilbert Dann abode I would call her, have her join me bag and baggage, and help me decide which bank we'd hit first.

I keyed myself in and automatically locked the three police locks behind me and walked into the living room and froze like an Eskimo Pie. Max Gantry was standing behind the black leather recliner easy chair, training a brightly polished automatic on my middle, his forefinger a whisper away from squeezing the trigger. The hooded look I had noticed around his eyes last night at the club was gone, and I didn't like in the least what I saw there today. I had seen that kind of gaze before, in the psycho ward of a hospital.

All my adult life I've envied the aplomb of characters in fiction and film who can wisecrack in the shadow of a pistol barrel: Welcome to my humble home. Like a glass of white wine before you kill me? I was terrified and consequently speechless, which meant that Max had to open the dialogue by default.

"I ought to shoot you in the guts right now, you fucking bastard. You and the bitch both."

"I don't . . . I don't . . ." was the best I could manage. I counted it a victory that I didn't foul my underwear.

"Shut up!" he screamed, all the suavity and control of Gantry the Teller of Riddles flown out the window. "Not one word out of your fucking mouth! Thought you were going to clean me out, didn't you? You and that cheap bitch! I set her up in a beautiful pad, give her clothes and jewels, and I was even gonna get her a BMW to drive, and all I ask is that she's *loyal* to me, that she's *faithful* to me. So what does she do? She fucks around with you the minute my back's turned, and the two of you decide you can clean out Max Gantry. You think I'm *blind* or something? Ten minutes after I walked into my office today I knew there was a fucking visitor last night. Goddamn amateur, take the calendar off the wall and put it back with September showing when it's been October for three weeks already!"

Stupid, stupid, *stupid*! I cursed myself. So that's how he knew.

"So when my boys told me there was no sign of forced entry I figured whoever it was had to have a key, and then I figured who coulda had a dupe made from my key ring, so Moose and I paid the bitch a little unannounced visit and after we worked on her fingers with a hammer she coughed up this address, so I left him to play with her and I came down here to settle with you. Do you know what I'm going to do with the two of you? I'm going to call the Moose and tell him to get the bitch ready for a trip, and then I'm going to call the club and have my limo pick the two of us up and then pick up Moose and the bitch, and we're all going to take a nice little drive to a quiet place I know in northwest Jersey, and I'm going to let the Moose have some fun with the bitch and you can watch him rip her in half and then you can watch me fix her face and tits with a carving knife. Then we'll work on you and the bitch can watch, if the eyeballs are still in her head."

His tirade might have made a commando quiver, but paradoxically it had the opposite effect on me. It gave me power. *He still doesn't know!* the voice told me. He has no idea who I am or who his erstwhile bedmate is or what we've been after, and thinks we were just out to loot some piddling wall safe in the club! I know something you don't know, I repeated to myself as the mystic transformation process went on, Gantry becoming weaker as I grew stronger, readier to take him. I had to take him. Either that or watch him twist my living entrails in his hands.

I waited till the madness in him had wound down and he was silent for a moment. "Are you through?" I asked him then. "Is it okay if I say something?"

He said neither yes nor no, just stood there shaking with fury.

"Mister, I don't know who you are and I don't understand a damn word you've said. As far as I'm concerned you're a sneak thief who broke in here and threatened me with a gun. If some chick you've been sleeping with is cheating on you, that's your problem, but if she told you that she and I are in some kind of plot together, well, whoever she is, she just gave you an address at random to take some heat off herself. I don't get involved in any arrangements with a woman, business or personal." I treated him to a parody limp-wrist gesture. "I'm gay, and proud as hell of it." With my mouth I kept up the rapid-fire patter and with my eyes I watched his eyes and waited for the first flicker of doubt to creep in, and the antic serendipitous part of my mind conjured up memories of those old Marx Brothers movies where a Groucho surrounded by hostile forces lets loose such a barrage of double-talk that he scrambles everyone's brains and escapes with hide intact. "But just because I'm gay doesn't mean I'm soft or a sissy, in fact I went through Ranger and airborne training and was an artillery observer in Nam for a year and half and—Look, I can prove what I say, I keep a scrapbook with pictures of all my lovers, it's on the floor underneath the couch." That was the moment. His eyes strayed down for a microsecond and my leg shot out like a Green Bay Packer kicking a field goal from the opposition's forty-five and the toe of my shoe caught him square on the kneecap and he howled and pitched sideways with the automatic still in his hand and I kicked it out of his hand and landed on top of him and banged his silly face into the parquet until it wasn't a face any more.

I hauled myself off him, gasping, my blood roaring. It was all I could do to keep from picking up the automatic and spattering his brains over the floor. I made myself stagger away from him until I'd recovered a modicum of control. Stumbled into the kitchenette and gulped a mouthful of Dewar's without benefit of a glass.

I found the roll of sturdy electrician's tape in the utility drawer and came back into the living room and bound Gantry's arms behind him in an impossible position. I wrapped tape around his bloody face like a black bandage, covering his eyes and mouth and leaving just enough of an opening around the nose so he had a fifty-fifty chance of not suffocating. I packed my Gilbert Dann clothes in the two-suiter, dragged Max into the bedroom closet, locked the closet door and, after I and my bag and his automatic were in the hall, locked the front door of the pad. Down on Ninth I whistled for a cab. "Over to First Avenue and uptown," I told the driver, who was young and black and sported a medium Afro and goatee and—thank heaven for affirmative action!—drove like Al Unser in the Indy 500.

Five blocks short of her building I told the kid to slow down and searched the street for a pay phone. Found one on the corner half a block from the apartment and on the same side of First. "Turn here," I said. "Park." I handed a pair of twenties across the back of the front seat. "Wait." I slammed the cab door behind me, fed a dime into the phone slot, and dialed her number and listened to it ring and ring. Twelve times, fifteen times . . . God, he'd said Moose was there with her and he'd said he was going to call Moose with instructions, which meant that he couldn't have told Moose not to answer the phone! So why the son-of-a-bitching hell doesn't he answer the phone?

On the twentieth ring it was picked up. "Yeah?" It was an ugly blunt sort of voice that comported well with my mental image of a three-hundred-pound bruiser with a face carved out of pork fat.

The ability to sound like other people is one of the

weapons in the first-class confidence person's arsenal, and although I wouldn't rank myself with Rich Little I am no slouch at the art. "It's me," I said, basing my Max Gantry imitation not on the maniac of this afternoon but rather on the suave performer of last night. "Is everything all right?"

"No sweat, chief," he grunted.

"You—hurt her any?"

"Naw, not since you left. She's meek as a lamb. Just crying up a storm, that's all."

My sigh of relief might have been heard across the Williamsburg Bridge. "Now get this straight," I told him. "Tie and gag her with a scarf or a slip or something, lock her in the john, and get out of that apartment. Right now. Go back to the club and wait for me in the office. I'll be there in about an hour. If I'm late, stay there until I come. Understood?"

"We, we ain't drivin' out to Joisy?" I could almost feel the disappointment in his voice. He was like a kid whose daddy wouldn't let him go see *Star Wars*.

"No," I told him forcefully, "we are not driving to Joisy."

"Well, why not?"

"Because the cops will be breaking down the door to that apartment in five minutes, you moron! Move your ass!" That was my Gantry Furioso imitation, based on my experience of the real thing less than an hour before, and if it didn't work I'd probably have to break in myself and kill the Moose with his boss's automatic. I slammed down the phone and trotted back to the cab and huddled in the far left corner of the passenger seat and stuck my head out the window, squinting along the building line to what I estimated was the doorway of her apartment house, counting off the seconds in my head. Minute and a half, minute and three quarters, *come on you goddamn lummox*!

"Hey, man." The cab jockey was twisted half around in the front seat like an overcooked pretzel and shaking me by the shoulder. "You a cop or something, mister?"

"Or something," I said mechanically. With my eyes still fixed on that doorway I groped for my wallet and found an appropriate card, which I handed to the kid.

The effect was way beyond what I had anticipated. "Ho-ly shit!" He whistled. "A real private eye! Hey, Mr. Lattman, how come none of you dudes ever has no sharp young black cat for an assistant?"

"What the hell do you think you're being right now?" My reply was tinged with miff and perhaps even a touch of irk: he was breaking my concentration. Two minutes and a quarter, two and a half . . . There he was, coming out of the doorway and looking up and down First Avenue as if he expected a copmobile any second. Unless there were two three-hundred-pound hulks on the way out of the same building at almost the same moment, it had to be Moose Eliot. He stuck out his fist to snare a passing cab, piled into the back seat, and shot out of my line of vision.

I glanced down at the plastic-framed ID card stuck to the back of my own cab's front seat. Xanthames J. Hanks, the driver's name was. "If you're going to be my sharp young assistant I ought to know what to call you," I told him.

"Just call me Zan, man," he drawled.

"Zan, will another twenty keep you parked here for, say, fifteen minutes longer?"

"For Arthur Lattman, you bet your ass it will."

I gave him the bill, slammed the cab door behind me, ran halfway up the block to the building. In the vestibule I pressed every buzzer in the double row until I heard the electric wheeze of the inner door lock being released. Her apartment was 3-B. I used the fire stairs to get me to the third floor and a handy-dandy skeleton key to get me past her front door. The place was dead empty, quiet as the tomb, but I didn't see any signs of violence. "It's me!" I roared. "Milo! Where the hell are you?"

"Mm hmmm hmmm mm hmmm!" I followed the muffled sounds into the bedroom, saw what looked like the door to the john at the far end. "Stand away if you can," I told her, and kicked the door in and threw back the shower curtain and there she was, lying on her side in the dry tub, her hands tied behind her with one scarf and her mouth stuffed with another and her eyes bulging with terror. I took the gag out of her mouth, lifted her out of the tub, and freed her hands. She fell against me clinging and sobbing and I soothed her and stroked her hair and told her everything was all right.

"They—they made me give them your—your address," she stammered. "Oh, God, my hand!" I took her right hand in my own. The fourth and fifth fingers looked horrible. I tried to touch them and she screamed.

"Did Gantry do this, or was it the Moose?" I asked her in a voice that sounded like nothing human.

"Moose held me. Max broke them."

"I broke him worse," I told her. "Come on, we have to get you to a doctor. Where's the bag I told you to pack this morning?"

"Hall . . . closet. Unless they took it with them."

"They didn't. What else do you need?"

"Handbag. Coat," she said through her pain.

I saw a roomy tan leather purse on the bed with its contents scattered all over the floor and scooped everything up and back inside while she held her right hand in her left and tried to hold in the sobs. With her purse and a light fall coat in one hand and her suitcase from the hall closet in the other I led her out of the apartment, hanging onto her arm as best I could in my loaded-down condition. The pain made her stagger like a drunk.

I opened the cab door for her, helped her in. "Okay, streetwise young assistant," I told the jockey. "This lady has two fingers broken. You find me a doctor who'll fix her up and keep his mouth shut."

"Leave it to Zan, man," he said, and gunned out of the parking space like a rocket from a cannon.

Less than an hour later the three of us were in some kind of office building in the upper reaches of Harlem with a gray-bearded black medic who had set her fingers in splints and wrapped them in gauzy bandages. Her eyes looked normal now, thanks to the anesthetic the old doc had shot into her. I passed out twenties to the two black men and joined them in a slug of el cheapo Scotch from the bottom shelf of a medical cabinet.

"Can she travel?" I asked the doctor.

"If you don't mind being conspicuous, I suppose she can." The old man nodded sagely at the cocoon of bandage around her fingers.

"All right, bright young assistant." I turned to Xanthames J. Hanks, who was taking advantage of my colloquy with the sawbones to help himself to another gulp of Scotch. "Want to earn another hundred tonight after you go off duty with the cab company?"

"Do I want another hundred?" His eyes took on a wolf look as he flashed his polished teeth at me. "Is this booze wet? Does Dolly Parton have tits? Does a dog piss at a lamppost?"

And so it came about that the two of us were driven out of Manhattan after dark in a late-model Cadillac, which our chauffeur swore had been borrowed with the owner's permission. We took the GW Bridge and various superhighways spanning New Jersey and then another bridge over the Delaware, and in the small hours of the night we said thanks and farewell to Zan the Man and entered the lobby of the Penn Central Hotel in beautiful downtown Philadelphia. As Mr. and Mrs. J. J. Gill we rented ourselves a suite and settled in to recuperate and plan the assault on Gantry's bank accounts.

SEVEN

During interscam sabbaticals I have killed many a long evening in the art house type of movie theater, and over the years I've developed a fondness for the Japanese cinema. My favorite among that country's directors is Kurosawa, but I am moved almost equally by the films of that less lionized master, Kenji Mizoguchi. Every time I see Mizoguchi's Ugetsu *I almost weep when Masayuki Mori turns to Machiko Kyo after a night of erotic splendor and says to her: "I never dreamed such pleasures existed!" Every man who has felt desire and loneliness wants someday to be able to say that honestly to a woman.*

Once I did.

From the notebooks of Milo Turner

There we were, my lady and I, momentarily secure in a luxurious hotel suite, with the chill of the night at bay and our whereabouts unknown to the world and nothing much to do except keep low profiles and think about all the money that was waiting for us to scoop it up. From a fiction writer's point of view, it would have been the perfect time and place for a sex scene. Except for two little glitches in the continuity: how do you make advances to a woman with two freshly mashed fingers, and how do you get over the strange illusion that she is more or less your sister?

What she needed was not a lover but a nurse. And so for the next week I mother-henned her, went out to local delicatessens and fast food emporiums for meals that I brought back for us to eat in our rooms, bought some paperbacks, which I read to her when she didn't feel like watching the tube, fed her the pain pills the doctor had given me for when the hand acted up on her, and took pleasure in watching her mend. We slept in the same bed, but virginally.

Until the night when something woke me and I yelped and reared half out of bed and then looked down at myself and saw that my pajama top was unbuttoned and her left hand, the undamaged one, was poised a few inches from my chest. I twisted around under the covers to face her. She was naked and sweetly scented and sitting up in bed, the nightgown that she'd worn when we'd said good night flung over a chair in the corner.

"Surprise, darling," she said softly. "Suddenly I'm feeling much better, so I decided it was time I made you feel good too."

And at that instant all the barriers crumbled and I reached for her and we kissed, long slow dreamy open-mouthed kisses while I stroked her glistening blond hair and her shoulders, and I held her away from me and gazed at her, and then kissed her again, first tenderly and then wildly, while she struggled to undress me and hurl my pajamas to the floor.

It may have been the hardest thing I have ever made myself do. I gently drew her hand away from me. "Are you sure this is what you want?" I whispered to her. "You don't owe me any favors."

She twined our fingers together and eased me down beside her so that our thighs touched. "You don't know how long and how much I've wanted you, darling. Ever since that first night on Madison when I stopped you on the street, I've been dreaming of this. Even when I was with Max, I pretended it was you. I want you as my teacher and I want you as my lover. Now, darling. Now."

She laid her hand on the back of my neck and drew my mouth to her goddess breasts.

The memory of that love night in room 1432 of the Penn Central Hotel I will take to my grave. The perfection of her lean smooth body, the ecstasy sounds, the miracle of resurrected desire as she made me come alive again and again. Somewhere in the gray dawn, just as we were drifting into well-earned naps, I noticed that she was fingertip-tracing a convolution of invisible lines on my belly. When she saw that I was still awake enough to notice she explained without my having to ask her.

"The weird patterns life makes," she said. "Fred and me, Fred and you, Fred and Max, Max and me, Max and you, you and me."

"Round and round, together bound," I said, half asleep.

"Hmm?"

"Truffaut," I mumbled. "*Jules and Jim.* Jeanne Moreau, Oskar Werner, and I forget the other guy's name. A song she sings in the movie."

"Good picture?"

"Damn good picture," I yawned.

"Will you take me to see it sometime?"

"If you like."

"I want you to be my teacher," she said. "I want you to teach me everything you know." And suddenly I wasn't sleepy anymore, and afterward the two of us were exhausted more than ever but we still didn't quite want to hang it up and sleep. We lay side by side and held hands in the ghostly gray dawn light and something flew out of a dark corner of memory into words before I could stop it.

"The very first time I saw you," I said, "when you were swimming all by yourself in that pool in Arizona, I had a fantasy, or a premonition, or something. Just for two or three seconds I knew that someday we were going to be together. God, I haven't thought about that since nineteen fifty-nine, and now it all comes true."

"The weird patterns life makes," she said again, and we dropped into the depths of sleep.

In the quiet interludes of our love time we came to know each other as neither of us had ever been known before. On the third night I followed the old black doctor's orders and took the bandages and splints off her fingers and she flexed them gingerly and grinned like a carefree child and held them out for me to kiss because they were the only part of her that so far I hadn't. And then we undressed each other and made slow quiet love, dream love, gentle and peaceful, that grew and transformed itself into wild passion and left us spent.

We allowed ourselves one more day and night of rapture before we got down to business.

Technically I suppose we had done some work on the project even during our honeymoon. I decided to junk my fantasy of crisscrossing the country and demolishing all eight of the accounts we had cracked and go for the prudent alternative of looting the single fattest account and then calling it quits. "There's just too much risk if we get greedy," I argued, not that she needed the hard sell. "Banks mail statements of account to their depositors every month. Gantry or Garza or whoever gets the mail at the accommodation address they're using receives twelve of those statements every thirty days at staggered intervals. We have no idea what time of the month the statement from any given bank goes out. But once the other side reads the first statement from a bank after we've hit the account, they'll know someone's into their system, and they'll probably send guns to all the other banks in the network and take us out when we make our next move. That's why we're not going to be hogs, darling."

"You're my guru," she said. "You call the play."

"The richest account is the one in Oregon. United States National Bank in Portland, under the name of Stephen K. Williston. Over nine hundred thou when Siegel checked it for me. Didn't Fred tell you that he had about twenty-five thousand dollars in each of his twelve hidey-holes, maybe three hundred thousand in all?"

"So one hit and we triple our money!" she crowed. "Or rather, I double mine and you pick up a third of a million for yourself. Good deal all around." She reached for my hand to squeeze it between hers. The fourth and fifth fingers of her right hand still didn't look right to me.

"Except for Gantry when Garza finds out he's been taken," I said.

We took a midmorning flight on Northwest from Philadelphia International Airport to Portland, charging the tab to the J. J. Gill credit card that had been financing us since we'd checked into the Penn Central Hotel. The flight took almost four hours real time but less than an hour zoned time: up into the clouds at eleven A.M., on the Portland tarmac before noon. Food was adequate, turbulence minimal. Our only gripe was the abominable in-flight movie. From the terminal we limoed to the Portlander Downtown Inn, which we'd chosen as our base camp because it was a few blocks' walk from the target.

First course on the menu was to reopen commo lines with the Jock. From a pay booth in a heavy-traffic office building lobby I dialed the appropriate numbers, identified myself, and brought that paragon of disembodied intelligence up to date on the adventures of myself and my sublime protégée.

"And ye didn't think to bring her with ye to the phone

so I could wish her me best? Milo, lad, 'tis sore disappointed in ye I am."

"I don't want a woman with two messed up fingers to be seen in public any more than necessary until I'm sure it's safe," I explained. "Which reminds me, what's happened to Gantry the past couple weeks? Did I kill the son-of-a-bitch?"

"Just put him in need of a plastic surgeon, so the word goes."

"Maybe next time. . . . All right, back to business. Jocko, I need someone who can outfit me with a few spare identities, the way Lafferty does when I work the East. Is Humpty Hackel still in that line?"

"I hope to tell ye! Still uses that passport photo place on Geary in San Francisco. A wise choice too, me lad. Next to me countryman Lafferty he's the best there is at the trade."

And so that afternoon, after telling my lady where I was bound and why, I traipsed back to the airport and snagged a commuter flight to the jewel city of northern California. My first stop was a savings and loan which shall be nameless, where I withdrew ten thousand dollars from one of my own retirement accounts and turned it into a cashier's check made out to bearer. My second and final stop was Humphrey Hackel Photomart, a hole-in-the-wall on Geary where I discovered that the West Coast's finest document forger was a bean pole with no chin and little hair and a wizardry with phony credentials whose like I had seldom encountered. I left his shop and hailed a cab back to the airport, my wallet bulging with proof that I was quite literally three other people.

Next day back in Portland I became one of the trio of newborn men and phoned for an appointment with a responsible officer of the United States National Bank. I was connected with a Mr. Dzergouski and kept my words over the wire crisp and lean. "Sir, my name is

John Hart, I'm a partner in the law firm of Moore and Hart here in the city, and our office has been retained by one of your large depositors—Mr. Stephen Williston of New York City?"

"I, ahhh, don't believe I've ever met Mr. Williston, but I am of course familiar with the name," the voice on the other end replied with a banker's excess of caution.

"Mr. Williston naturally does all his banking in Portland by mail," I said. "But there seems to be a problem with his account. He has retained our office to look into what he claims were three unauthorized withdrawals in the past nine months. If his allegations are correct, our office is empowered to bring an action against U.S. National for the missing funds, on the ground that you negligently honored forged withdrawal orders."

"Oh, shit," I distinctly heard Mr. Dzergouski mutter sotto voce.

"Could I see you about this matter as soon as possible?" I requested in my best this-can-surely-be-settled-without-a-lawsuit manner.

I was in his office at three thirty that afternoon. After twenty minutes of earnest conversation Dzergouski buzzed his secretary and told her to drop what she was doing and make him a Xerox copy of each monthly statement on the Williston account since January first, and of each deposit and withdrawal slip for the year as well.

"Um-hrmm," I butted in. "Perhaps a copy of Mr. Williston's original signature card when he opened the account would also help."

Dzergouski bobbed his leonine head in agreement and added that item to the photocopy order. He was terrified of a lawsuit and practically tripping over his shoelaces in his eagerness to straighten out the mess amicably. While we were waiting for the copies, I tried to de-stress the fancy-suited limp-wit by mentioning casually that Mr. Williston was over seventy and, well, possibly just a bit inclined to be forgetful, and Dzergouski gravely acknowledged that, yes, these little problems were to be expected after a certain age, and then segued into an interminable anecdote about his doddering mother-in-law. When the secretary deposited the photocopied documents on his blond wood desk, we bent over to scrutinize the signatures, and after the study ritual I judiciously concurred in the banker's judgment that superficially at least they all looked genuine.

"I'll call Mr. Williston tonight and question him closely," I promised, "but if you haven't heard from me by tomorrow afternoon you'll know the whole thing's been a false alarm. Very nice meeting you, Mr. Dzergouski. Hope your wife's mother gets over her problem." I shook his hand and walked out of the United States National Bank's main office with copies of every document I wanted in my neat leather attaché case.

I had to restrain myself from dancing up the street Fred Astaire–style as I beelined for the Portlander Downtown Inn. According to the latest monthly statement, which had gone out earlier that week, the current balance in the account was $978,633.56, a gain of almost fifty thou from the figures Marty Siegel had given me. And to frost the cake even more scrumptiously, the date on that statement meant that it would be another three and a half weeks before the next one would be sent out and spill the news to Gantry and Garza that someone had busted their piggy bank.

My occupation for the next several days was sedentary. I sat in our hotel room practicing the Stephen K. Williston signature as Fred Schuyler had written it God knew how many years ago, until early the following week, I was satisfied I could write that name in my sleep. Now it was time to activate Hackel Identity Number

Two, which by a curious coincidence happened to be in the name of Stephen K. Williston. I took the ten-thousand-dollar-cashier's check I had picked up on my whirlwind trip to San Francisco and used it to start my own Williston account in the Merchants Bank of Oregon. The next few days my love-dove and I spent most of our time indoors, wallowing by day in the cultural splendor of Portland TV, pleasuring each other by night. On Monday I paid a midmorning visit to Merchants Bank, identified myself as Stephen K. Williston, and asked to see a vice pres. The one they steered me to was a pigeon of the first water. I told him how pleased I was at the services offered by his own mighty institution and how miffed I had become at U.S. National, where I maintained a much larger account. When with my consent he put in a call to his counterpart at U.S. National and found out exactly how many Willistonian greenbacks were on deposit there, he sat up straighter in his posture chair, smiled a bit more broadly, adjusted the knot of his tie to a choking position. He was a banker scenting business. On the basis of my alleged interest in moving all my Portland money to Merchants, he treated me to a lavish lunch crowned with Courvoisier at his posh and snobby club. Afterward, back in his office, I filled out the paperwork for a wire transfer of funds, which means an order to U.S. National to pay over the entire proceeds of its account in the name of Stephen K. Williston to the Merchants account in the same name.

Such are the joys of the confidence person's life. When I left Merchants late that afternoon I was just short of a million dollars richer than when I'd walked in. On the way back to the Portlander I stopped at the Wine Cask and bought a bottle of the house's finest, and my lady and I celebrated victory all the rest of that day and deep into the night.

Just before we collapsed into sleep we had some pillow

talk. I thought that was the best time, after good wine and love, to tell her that I was revising our business arrangement. "I'm not going to take a third of it," I insisted quietly. "Just my expenses, around fifty thou, I figure. All the rest is yours."

"Darling, that's sweet of you and I really appreciate it, but I want you to have your share," she said. "In fact, I want you to take half."

"I thought we agreed when we went into this deal that I'd call the shots."

"And you have been, love. All the way."

"Then please let me divide the jackpot as I see fit, will you? Let's say nine hundred thousand for you and the rest for me. That's almost eighty thousand, which is a lot more than my expenses."

Her voice took on a hard edge of the sort that I find distasteful in beautiful women. "One third for you and the rest for me," she said. "That gives me more than six hundred thousand dollars as my share—and remember, Fred told me that there was about twenty-five thousand dollars in each of his twelve accounts, or three hundred thousand all told, so I've more than doubled my legacy and I certainly don't need more than that for my nest egg. Let's—well, let's just call the rest of it Fred's legacy to you."

"You know what Fred's real legacy to me is?"

"No," she said curiously. "What?"

"You are," I said, and held her close again. "And the dear old man never knew it, either."

The next morning, hollow-eyed but still ecstatic, we took a commuter bird to San Francisco, checked in at the Mark Hopkins under the third identity I'd purchased from Humpty Hackel, and spent a week juggling bank orders so that the $978,000 in the Williston account at Merchants Bank of Portland was systematically and untraceably scattered into a melange of other accounts under Milonic control. Then we booked ourselves on a series of hopscotch flights, stopping off in L.A., Phoenix, and Dallas, so that I could set up a $200,000 account under a freshly minted female name in a bank in each city, using funds from one of my own retirement accounts in a different bank in the same metropolis. The balance of her two-thirds share, which came to almost sixty thousand bivalves, she took in cash and traveler's checks. Argue with her as I would, she was stone adamant about not accepting a penny more.

The operation was over. We spent one extra night in Dallas, and there was a sadness about our coupling, because even though neither of us said a word about it we both knew it was the end of a very special time in our lives and we couldn't know if it would ever come again. We kissed good-bye at the airport next morning and promised to stay in touch through the Jock and left that city of heartbreak on separate flights and in different directions. Mine was due north, to Toronto.

Forty thousand feet above the earth I leaned back in my plane seat and stared out the plastic window at cloud formations that looked like cotton candy and thought about her. About the respite from bottomless loneliness that she'd brought to me, about the feeling I couldn't shake that Fred from his grave had appointed me her new father protector as well as her lover. About the certainty I felt in my blood and bones that she was just too sweet and giving a person to have a chance in hell of making a success of the life.

My flight to Canada had an intermediate stop in Minneapolis. I took myself and my two-suiter off the plane and didn't bother to come back. I taxied downtown, checked into a hotel, and spent the next two days doing some more fund juggling, enriching each of her three new bank accounts by a hundred thousand dollars.

"You need the cushion, my love," I told her invisible presence in my lonely bed, "and you'll never have to sleep with a man you don't care for to keep yourself alive. Never again."

The next time we met, if we ever did meet again, I wondered if she would hate me.

EIGHT

My favorite novelist is Dickens. Not only because he created a legion of marvelous characters, not only for the perfect balance he kept between a realistically cynical worldview and his soaring romanticism. I love Dickens most of all because, like myself, he plotted with glee. He wasn't afraid to build his masterpieces on interlocking networks of coincidence that would choke a horse, because he knew that bizarre coincidences are the stuff of everyday life.

My life too.

From the notebooks of Milo Turner

The last time I saw her was just a week before the night I opened the paper in the Fireside Inn and saw that she was dead.

Six years older and several dozen identities wiser than when she and I had first come together in New York, I was back in the city on another of my George Boyd sabbaticals. After the raid on his laundry for mob money, Max Gantry had dropped, as far as anyone could tell, down a bottomless pit, and the rumor was that Angelo Garza had exacted a due and awful vengeance on his bod before releasing him to Mister Death. The Matchwit Club had been turned into a pizzeria.

I spent my mornings in the sun-bright den of my Central Park South condo, composing epigrams for my notebooks. Afternoons were devoted to culture-sipping, in multilevel bookstores with speaker systems tuned to WQXR, in art galleries awash with high-priced color blobs that could have been thrown on the canvas by a troop of monkeys, in intimate little movie houses that ran retrospectives of the great directors. Evenings were for the pleasure of the table and the bed. I vegetated.

That Friday night was too raw and wet for an indoorsman. I reheated half a leftover quiche for dinner, played Shostakovich's score for the Soviet movie of *Hamlet* on my stereo, browsed through the magnificent color plates in Walter Kaufmann's *Religions in Four Dimensions.* The storm died away a little before eleven and I decided to break my cabin fever, exit my high-rise haven, and take a nice little walk.

There is something unearthly about the nightscape of a great city after rain. Puddles mirror the street and building lights. Avenues empty of traffic point uptown like glistening black arrows. I breathed cool wind in my face as shadows danced over the pools of light. My route was impromptu: Central Park South to Madison, north into the Sixties, east to Second, south a few blocks, then west on Fifty-seventh. That was when I decided I was a tad thirsty and thought about stopping for a nightcap if I could find a quiet bar. I began studying the buildings along the block and, just a few doors ahead of me, saw what looked like a cozy cave. There was a woman just coming out of the doorway.

Her.

A convergence of that sort cannot possibly be planned, but once it happens you can't help but believe that it was *meant.* If she'd lingered over her drink half a minute longer or had taken a few seconds less time to settle with the barman, or if I'd chosen to cross town on Fifty-eighth or Fifty-sixth, or maybe even if I hadn't been on the lookout for a waterhole at that precise moment, we wouldn't have run into each other.

Our casual glances locked, and her eyes and I suppose mine too went bulgy with amazement and delight, and then we were kissing and hugging and making little squeals of pleasure and being very careful to keep it on a darling and lover basis because after all we were in the open and neither of us knew what name the other might be using.

"I have the feeling this has all happened before," she whispered.

"It did," I said. "October seventy-six, remember? God, it's been a long time." I stepped back a few paces to look at her, head to toe. "Lovely as ever," I told her.

"I'm well over thirty now," she reminded me.

"And I'm well over forty, so you're still a child to me. Did—those fingers heal okay?" I had never got over my guilt twinges about that: if not for my own stupidity putting the Perry calendar back on the wall with the wrong month showing, it would never have happened.

"I had to have them reset but they're all right now. Oh, it's so good seeing you! I had no idea you were back in New York."

"The Jock could have told you, if you'd kept in touch with him. And he could have told me you were in town too."

"I know. I'm sorry, darling, I've been terribly thought-less, but I've always been frightened of how much that man or mind or whatever he is knows, and I just phys-ically couldn't pick up the phone and routinely tell him where I was and what I was doing. Forgive me?"

"For anything."

"If you're not too sleepy I do want to talk with you. Something extremely important." She lowered her voice to an almost inaudible murmur full of promise. "My place is only a few blocks from here."

That was the last coherent sentence either of us spoke for the next few hours. And ah, was I happy I'd decided to stretch my legs. She led me into the bedroom of her cozy apartment in an old building in the mid Fifties and we undressed and adjourned to the shower and cavorted in the warm and tingly spray. Afterward she rubbed herself all over with baby oil, and when neither of us could wait another second we collapsed onto her bed and threw the covers off and I lay on my back on the cool sheets and she knelt before me and danced with her breasts and belly and at long last slid down upon me and moaned and trembled in an all but epileptic fit of ecstasy. We lay together half dead with exhaustion and snuggled and shared pillow talk for a few minutes before we drifted into dreamland in each other's arms.

And in the pitch-dark hour before dawn, the dead time when men and women torn apart with loneliness have to fight the urge to slit their wrists, we came awake and found ourselves ravenously hungry and went out to her neat little kitchenette and made ourselves coffee and a monster Spanish omelet, which we took to her breakfast nook. We sat, and I lifted my stoneware mug in a ceremonial toast to our reunion.

"Wait a minute." She got up and crossed the living room to a low walnut cabinet near the fake fireplace and slid back its door. Even from across the room I could make out a row of bottles of the exotic liqueurs that were her favorite tipple. She picked one fat little soldier from the row and brought it back to the breakfast table. It wasn't liqueur but an excellent brandy. She poured generous shots into our coffee mugs. "Now it's a real toast," she said.

"To you. Love, peace, health, fortune. The satisfaction of your every wish. The fulfillment of your every need. Forever." We clinked cups, somewhat more awkwardly than our bodies had come together.

"And all of those to you even more," she said.

Then we dug into the omelet before it turned cold. It was the first meal she had cooked for me, and a splendid debut it was. As I ate and watched her across the table, her golden love-tousled hair and love-swollen lips put all sorts of subversive thoughts in my brain. Premature retirement. Permanent residence in the George Boyd persona with my sweet lady beside me. Abandoning the life and my small army of identities for domesticity and quiet contentment. Well, why not? Hadn't even the King Fox retired early? Maybe that's what he would have wanted me to do, hang it up and start over with her on the proceeds earned to date.

With our omelet demolished I decided to very gingerly test the waters, sound her out, and I was formulating a casual query about the current balance in her accounts when she beat me to the punch. "Milo," she said, "is it all right if we talk now? I do have something very important to tell you, and it's going to take a while."

I could almost hear the moment go *bang* and explode like a burst balloon. "Whatever you want," I said quietly.

"I guess I should begin with a confession. Darling, I've been a miserable washout in the life. I hoped that knowing you and learning from you would, well, improve my luck or my skill or whatever. But it hasn't helped a bit. At least, not till recently."

Confirming a prediction I had made but suppressed half a dozen years ago. "I'm sorry I didn't have a better effect on you," I said. "But thank heaven I started those accounts for you after the bank scam."

"Oh, Milo, there's almost nothing left in them! Some of it I . . . well, I gave away. There was a shelter for battered women and then there was a little girl who had third-degree burns all over and the insurance company refused to pay for all the skin grafts she needed. . . . I just keep running into people I have to help. And what was left over—well, this is embarrassing as hell, darling, but I was conned out of almost a hundred thousand last year. My own dumb fault too. So the bottom line is that there isn't a whole lot of money left."

Those subversive thoughts were crawling across my brain again, stronger than ever. Maybe she was ready for early retirement too. I wondered if I dared suggest the possibility to her.

"But if the operation I'm working now pays off," she went on, "all the ones that blew up in my face won't matter. Oh, Milo, it *has* to pay! I'm half climbing the walls with excitement and half scared to death. Okay if I tell you about it? You're sure you're not too sleepy?"

"I'm wide awake," I lied. "What's your scam?"

"What do you know about Haskell's Supermarkets?" she asked me.

Frequent traveler over the length and breadth of the nation that I am, the question didn't faze me. "It's a chain of stores. Runs all over the Midwest, as far as I know. They're all built alike, red brick front with a sort of fake Roman arch over the entrance."

"Do you know anything about how the chain began?"

"Never had the slightest interest."

"It was started by Bradford Haskell right after World War Two ended," she told me, "and supermarkets were eating up the mom-and-pop grocery stores practically overnight. Haskell was married in nineteen forty-eight, but all he lived for was building up a supermarket empire. He treated his wife like garbage. She left him early in nineteen fifty. She was pregnant at the time but didn't know it yet and didn't tell him when she found out. The kid was born later in fifty, a daughter. She named her Ann. Her divorce from Haskell became final in nineteen fifty-one. He never saw her again and never saw his child even once. He wasn't interested, he was too busy making millions of dollars as the Supermarket King of the Midwest."

"The glory of the free enterprise system," I said. "There's no limit to how much you can make if you're obsessive enough. Okay, so what happened next?"

"A few years later Haskell married again. This time he made more of a success of it. He had two sons by the second wife. The older boy is named Jeffrey. He's currently employed as chief of the legal department of Haskell's Markets Incorporated. The younger kid, Gene, is a third violinist with the Saint Louis Symphony Orchestra. Their mother, the second Mrs. Haskell, died of cancer ten years ago. The old man is living now in a beautiful mansion in Ladue, which is a ritzy suburb about half an hour's drive from downtown Saint Louis. He's had several heart attacks lately and the doctors' prognosis is that he won't live out the year."

"You seem to have done a lot of research," I complimented her.

"Research, hell! I just got back last Sunday from a two-week stay with those people. You see, my dear," she said proudly, "I am Ann Haskell."

And for a minute there I almost believed her.

How my lady had acquired that identity would make an excellent flashback scene, but our narrative has already been encumbered with a blast from the past and my aesthetic sense dictates that I reduce this one to a quick summation. The gist of the story was that two years ago, between scams and at liberty in San Francisco, she had rented an apartment overlooking the bay and struck up a friendship with the young woman down the hall, who was calling herself Ann Montgomery. Ann was a very lonely and talkative lush, desperately in need of a sympathetic ear, which my lovebird was willing as usual to provide. Soon the drinking lady was confiding the sad tale of her life: that her real name was Ann Haskell, that she was the daughter of Bradford Haskell the Supermarket King, and that she lived for the day when they would shovel into the ground her unspeakable toad of a father, who had driven Ann's poor mother to an early grave, for on that day she would enter the city of Saint Louis in triumph and claim for herself a sizable chunk of the family fortune.

"She didn't make it. One night early last year she got herself drunk as a skunk and drove her car off the top of a mountain. She was thrown clear, so she didn't burn to death when the gas tank caught fire, but she broke her neck in the fall and died instantly. Some old farmer in a pickup truck was the first on the scene. He drove to the nearest phone and called the highway patrol and the nearest hospital, but he also called me, because Ann had me listed on a card in her wallet as the person to be informed in case of emergency." She stopped, poured more coffee on top of the dregs in her mug. "Milo, do voices ever talk to you? Tell you to do things that any outsider would say were crazy?"

"Once in a while. Remember the Matchwit Club?"

"I heard one of those voices as soon as I hung up the phone. I was sort of numb with the shock, but that voice was as loud and clear as yours is now. It told me to go down the hall to Ann's apartment and use a credit card to slip the lock." She must have seen my face fall with shock and distaste, because she quickly corrected my misinterpretation. "Oh, I didn't rob her, darling, you know me better than that! All I took out of there was every bit of evidence I could find that proved she was Bradford Haskell's daughter. Letters, photographs, some diaries that Ann's mother kept for a while, that sort of thing. As far as I know I got every item Ann had squirreled away for when she'd claim her share of her father's estate. She was buried as Ann Montgomery. I wound up paying for most of the funeral."

"And then you came back to New York . . . ?"

"And set up a life for myself as Ann Haskell, so that once they bury that old bastard I can go to Saint Louis and claim Ann's share of his money."

"Magnificent," I said, meaning both my lady and her scam, and lifted my long-empty coffee mug in friendly salute. "But darling, haven't you, er, overlooked something fairly crucial?"

"What are you talking about, Milo?"

"It's a fundamental principle of American law," I said, "and another of the glories of the free enterprise system, that no one is obligated to leave a child a cent in his will. In Europe it's different, they've got a concept called *légitime,* which means you can't disinherit any of your kids, and I believe they have the *légitime* in Louisiana because the laws down there are based on the Napoleonic Code. But everywhere else in this country a parent can cut a child out of his will for any reason at all, or no reason. How do you know Bradford Haskell didn't cut Ann out of his? After all, Ann's mother had run out on him in nineteen fifty and he never saw his child by her until Ann—er, that is, until you visited him in Saint Louis recently."

"That's just why I visited him," she said, "to find out about his will."

Oh you poor innocent child, I thought. Investing almost two years in an identity on the gamble that Ann Haskell was remembered in her old man's will.

"And I learned that he's left me a bundle," she went on blithely, unaware of the ass-backward nature of her strategy. "I've always been a big legatee in his will. The old goat had guilt feelings, I guess. Anyway, as the will now reads, I take one third of the residuary estate after taxes and some charitable bequests. By my calculations the residue is worth approximately ten million dollars. And now that Haskell has met me and likes me it's not very likely that he'll change the will to cut me out."

"You don't think your half brothers will try to poison the old man's mind against you?"

"Gene wouldn't. He's a nice sensitive artistic kid who wouldn't hurt a fly. I suppose some people would call him a wimp, and he has a few mannerisms that sort of signal that he might be gay, but I don't think he is. He's engaged to a young woman lawyer, one of those lean, wire and whipcord bitches. I hope he breaks up with her."

"How about the other son? Jeffrey?"

"Jeff is the spitting image of his father and his brother's girl. He's a pushy hard-driving castrating workaholic who's out first last and always for number one. I could see him trying to pressure old Haskell into cutting me out, but I don't think there's enough time left for him to have a chance."

"But you're sure they all accept you as the real Ann Haskell?"

"Bradford is dying," she said, "and wants to be forgiven for the way he treated Ann's mother. Gene is too naive to dream I could be a fake. Jeff isn't. He told me flat out before I left Saint Louis that he was going to have private detectives investigate me."

"That doesn't bother you?"

"I expected it. That's why I lived as Ann Haskell for so long before I made my move. I've even made some money as Ann, doing free-lance writing, magazine fillers and greeting card verses and stuff like that, just so Ann would have an open and aboveboard source of income."

"Has anything happened to make you think that detectives are checking you out?"

"Actually, darling, I half believe I've been shadowed off and on this week. Not tonight, though. I looked around very very carefully before I brought you up here. But three or four times earlier in the week I've noticed this strange man hanging around nonchalantly at different places I've been."

"What does he look like?"

"Tall, thin. He wears his hair in a widow's peak that's shaped exactly like the letter *M*. He could be Jeff's private detective or maybe he's just some creep who's trying to work up the guts to make a pass at me. I'm not worried about detectives, dear. My cover is perfect."

"Then why," I asked her, "are you scared half to death?"

The question hit home. It seemed to remind her of whatever it was that the effort of telling me her story in a coherent manner had shoved to the back of her mind. All of a sudden she was shivering and hugging herself as if the May morning had been a bitter January. I raced to the bedroom to bring her the hooded all-weather coat that she'd thrown down there with the rest of her clothes, but I almost didn't make it because I was going too fast and skidded for a second on the throw rug near the fake fireplace in the living room. I yipped, flung up my hands for balance, just barely kept on my feet. Went on into the bedroom and returned with her coat and draped it over the paper-thin peignoir she was wearing. When she had it buttoned and belted she answered my question in a voice so weak I could hardly hear her.

"I've been having premonitions," she said. "That somebody-walking-over-my-grave feeling. I don't know, maybe I'm frightened of success." She laughed nervously and pulled the coat tighter around herself. "Anyway, when we ran into each other I decided there must have been a reason why, and that's why I've been telling you this long-drawn-out story."

"In case something . . . happens to you?"

"I guess so." She scraped her chair over until it was

touching mine and she took my hand between hers. "Oh, Milo, this is so big and so important and I've had rotten luck so many times before and I can't think of anything that could possibly go wrong this time but I can't see myself making it, either." Gently she started to get up, her rising movement taking me with her. "Darling, please take me back to bed and just hold me close."

So we lay and cuddled for a while and napped for a bit, until in the raw gray Saturday morning before normal people were stirring I made myself disentangle from her and kissed her hair and eyes so lightly she didn't even wake. I found a sheet of paper and scrawled a note, which I left on the pillow where she'd find it. "Dearest: Just in case you are being watched by detectives, don't try to get in touch with me till it's over. Good luck forever. M. PS: Don't forget to tear up this note!" And I slipped out of her bedroom and her apartment and out of her life. The last glimpse I had of her she was sleeping there peacefully, curled up in an almost fetal position.

That next week was a busy one for me as I baited the hook for the murder-minded fat politico from North Jersey, but even if I had been at leisure I would have made it a point not to call or see her, because as I'd indicated in my note, if a private snoop were checking her out and found me in the picture it would screw up her scam royally. I had inadvertently done that to her once, in those long-ago days when I was the Reverend Doctor Callixtus Huckaby and she was running a Fundamentalist radio talk show in central Kansas, and I was damned if I'd risk doing it twice, even though I ached to see her again.

Wednesday morning I scanned the morning *Times* as usual when I'm residing in New York. On the obit page near the back of section one was an uncommonly interesting half column. BRADFORD W. HASKELL, 72, it was headed, FOUNDER OF SUPERMARKET CHAIN. Mr. Haskell had suffered a massive coronary and died at Barnes Hospital in Saint Louis just after 7:00 P.M. Tuesday. The article briefly recounted how in the boom years following World War II Mr. Haskell had entered the supermarket business and begun to build an empire that at its peak consisted of more than two hundred establishments in seven midwestern states, each of them instantly recognizable to the shopper by the Haskell's logo and the red brick front and Romanesque arch over the entranceway. Mr. Haskell had been married twice but both wives had predeceased him. He was survived by Ann, a daughter by his first wife, and by Jeffrey and Eugene, the sons by his second. Funeral arrangements were to be private.

That afternoon I dropped into a gift shop and picked out a little victory present for my lady. It was a cut-glass decanter partitioned into four segments, each intended to hold a liqueur of a different color. In the package store next door I bought bottles of four liqueurs whose shades, I thought, would blend well with each other: white crème de cacao, crème de menthe, Galiano, blue curacao. Then, because the decanter was more of a display item than a drink dispenser, I added to the order a bottle of Sabra, a chocolate and orange flavored Israeli liqueur that is one of my own favorites and that I hadn't noticed in her cabinet.

I had a strange dream Thursday night. I dreamed that they had given her the three and a third mil from Bradford Haskell's residuary estate and that we were together again somewhere, celebrating her triumph and retirement and the beginning of our new life. I poured out Sabra in two delicate liqueur glasses and brought them to the bed where she was naked and waiting, and she knelt on the bed and raised her arms over her head and bent forward and bathed her nipples in the Sabra and lay back and I lowered myself to her and licked the sweet liqueur from her breasts and we made love. It was one of those vivid and powerful dreams that force you awake and leave you gasping.

And then the weekend came, and I bussed over to Jersey to my dinner at the Fireside Inn with the tubby councilman who wanted a brother official erased, and I picked up that goddamn newspaper and read that goddamn obituary for Ann Haskell. And I could still almost see her beautiful image beside my own in the blackness of the window glass of the 35E bus as it ran headlong toward the symphony of lights that was New York.

NINE

Hammett in The Maltese Falcon *said it best, and the entire movie genre known as* film noir *is built on that perception. The world is a place where beams fall, out of nowhere, for no reason, and crush whoever happens to be standing in the wrong spot beneath them. One person may be smashed to a pulp, and another just a few inches away doesn't get a scratch. Life is horrible, wretched, disgusting, unfair. Any god that could have made the world what it is must be a malignant thug. We are abandoned to the whims of chance.*

So why do I still seek rational design?

From the notebooks of Milo Turner

When you are by nature a loner and your life has been a dance of juggled identities and the only person with whom you might have been able to share grief has just been snatched away from you, how do you mourn?

When the bus squealed to a stop at the top of one of the concrete ramps at Port Authority I stumbled out and escalatored down to the main floor and flagged a cab at the Eighth Avenue entrance and rode out of the Times Square combat zone. With sixty hundred-dollar bills in my pigskin I retained that much presence of mind. I paid off the driver at Central Park South, walked the block to the George Boyd condo, stayed just long enough to hide the money and bolt half a water-glassful of

Scotch. Then I went down to the street again and started walking.

I walked in patterns, squares and diagonals and rectangles and twisted figures geometry has no names for. Lines traced on my belly. *The weird patterns life makes.* East to Lex, north, east to Second, south, west to Madison, north again. Fast as my legs would power me through the night streets. Remembering. Trying to forget. Railing at the nothingness that had taken her from me into its own stinking embrace. I walked those impossible patterns for most of the night. It was almost as if I were tempting fate, daring some mugger to try and knock me off. If he did, either he would kill me and it would be over or I would rip his guts out with my teeth and bare hands and maybe somehow feel better. No one even came near me. The beams weren't falling in my neighborhood that night.

Sometime after four in the morning I groped my way back to the Central Park South condo, exhausted and footsore and ready to sell my soul for sleep. It came only in snatches, a ragged parody of rest that was haunted by dreams of the way it had been when she was alive.

A little before ten A.M. I gave up. Dragged myself out of bed, stood under alternating hot and cold showers, tried not to look at my devil face in the mirror while I shaved. Made a pot of double-strength coffee, drank four cups, munched on zwieback and Monterey Jack. And somewhere during the cycle of life-goes-on rituals to which I subjected myself, I began to think again.

Around noon, with the first wave of grief behind me and my brain in gear, I touch-toned the special number and broke the news of her death to the Jock.

"Ah, no," he said, his voice quiet but full of unspoken pain. "Ah, Milo, no. I never heard her voice once but ye've told me so much of her over the years that I came to think of her as one of me own. To have meant so much to you she must have been a bright and loving one indeed."

"I'll never know anyone like her again," I said. "There's nothing left for me now. Nothing to live for except finding the people who murdered her."

"Murdered? Murdered her, did ye say?" There was surprise in the cracked Dublin brogue, and I detected more than a trace element of disbelief too. "Now, be careful, me lad. From the facts in the newspaper story as ye gave them to me I heard not a thing that suggests foul play. When ye say she was murdered, mightn't it be the grief talking and not the common sense?"

"No, God damn it, it is not the grief talking!" That was the first time in my life that I have ever shouted at the Jock. "Look, I'll prove to you I'm thinking straight. I'll give you a reason for believing it was just an accidental fall that wasn't in the paper and that no one could know about but me. Just a week ago I almost slipped on that throw rug in front of her fireplace myself." I told him the story quickly. He waited till I was done before he made any comment, and when he did it was a question.

"And even in the light of that incident ye still maintain the poor girl's death isn't what it seems?"

"Damn well told, I do. Fact one. The newspaper quoted the cop in charge as saying she'd been drinking to excess Thursday night. Jocko, I've been with her when we had a lot to celebrate. Never once did she drink more than she could handle. Why should she have gotten pie-eyed Thursday night?"

"Because Bradford Haskell was dead and her scam was most of the way home?" the voice of pure intelligence suggested softly.

"Haskell died Tuesday evening. His obit was in Wednesday morning's *Times*. If she was going to get drunk it would have been Wednesday, not Thursday."

"Could she not have drunk too much Wednesday night as well?" the Jock asked.

"Fact two. The newspaper said her body was discovered shortly before nine Friday morning. How is that possible if she died accidentally and alone?"

"Could not a neighbor in her building have heard the crash of her fall and called the local precinct station?"

"*The next morning?* Jocko, by then she'd been dead for hours! Why didn't the neighbor call right away, if that's what happened? Why wait till daylight?"

"Proceed with your case," Jock said, like a trial judge admonishing counsel.

"Fact three. Bradford Haskell died Tuesday evening. The timing of the two deaths is just too damn close to be coincidence."

"Oh, ye don't believe coincidences happen, is that it? Ah, Milo, if chance were taken out of the world we wouldn't recognize the place. Listen, boy. Not ten minutes ago ye were telling me about the glorious happenstance of your seeing your lady again on Fifty-seventh Street a week ago Friday. That coincidence ye swallow without difficulty, and the much lesser coincidence of the father and daughter dying forty-eight hours apart makes ye gag?"

"I can't help it, Jock," I said. "I can't believe that . . . that it just happened."

"So what *do* ye believe? That one of Haskell's sons decided to kill the woman he thought was his half sister and increase his own share of the old man's estate from a third to a half?"

"Either that, or both brothers were in it together," I suggested.

"Milo, lad. Be reasonable for just a few moments, just as a favor to the old Jock, will ye, please? Now I have no law degree and nor do you but we both have our mother wit. Remember that your lady was alive at the time of

Bradford Haskell's passing. Doesn't that qualify her as the taker of the one third share that his will leaves her?"

I thought back over the fragments of legal learning I had accumulated during certain prior operations. "I suppose it does," I conceded.

"So once the old man was dead," the Jock went on, "it was too late for the sons to increase their shares that way!"

"Maybe," I argued, "they didn't know that."

"Milo, Milo! One of the sons is the head of the legal department of Haskell's Supermarkets. As a practicing attorney he surely would know this simple point of law."

"Okay, okay. So it was the other one who killed her. Gene, the violinist."

"A symphony orchestra musician flies in from Saint Louis with virtually no preparation and acting on a gross mistake about the law, and commits a murder so perfect it fools the New York City police? Son, take the old fool's advice. Leave Manhattan. Find an island far away. Drown the grief. Take up with another woman."

"Jock," I told him furiously, "you go directly to hell." And I slammed down the phone and stumbled to the kitchen to reheat what was left of the pot of double-strength coffee. I poured the dregs into my cup and fished in the bar cabinet for bourbon to add to the black brew, when I remembered the way she'd added brandy to our coffee in the hour before dawn eight mornings ago and flung the bottle aside.

It took me the rest of that unbearable day to figure what I was going to do next. I called Lafferty around eight that evening and made a date to visit Minetta Street the next morning. Then I spent an hour sipping Dewar's on rocks and listening to violin sonatas on WNCN and letting myself slowly wind down. The process worked too well. I went over the edge into sleep right there on my couch, and woke up after midnight feeling like a sackful of doorknobs. Undressed, fell into bed, blanked out again in less than a minute. The dreams I dreaded never came.

Be what you want to be, says the advertising jingle. Thanks to a long Sunday session at Lafferty's identity bazaar, I left the Central Park South condo after breakfast Monday morning with a borrowed leather attaché case monogrammed C.B.B. in gold lettering and a host of credentials asserting that my name was Charles Blackburn and my home base Saint Louis and my racket the learned profession of law. The paperwork was superb, down to a half used round-trip TWA ticket from Lambert International Airport to LaGuardia in the Blackburn name. Having forked over half of Fatso's six-thousand-dollar hit fee advance to Lafferty so that he'd outfit me on short notice, I felt I was entitled to the best. Nothing less, I believed, would suffice. The people I was out to fool were cops.

The neighborhood where Ann Haskell had lived and died was served by a precinct station housed in a three-story structure of glass and steel that looked no different on the outside from many a civilian business building. A uniform escorted me upstairs to the detective division on the top floor and handed me over to a tall and deeply tanned and outrageously handsome young hunk who sat soldier straight behind a steel desk adorned with a phone, a two-tiered correspondence basket, a pile of neatly aligned manila folders, and at one corner a stack of thick books with notation slips sticking out in profusion. The uniform introduced us. "Sergeant Domjan. Ted, this is Mr. Blackburn, a lawyer from Saint Louis. He wants to talk to someone about the Ann Haskell thing."

I shifted the attaché case to my left hand and offered my right. "Charles Blackburn," I said.

The young sergeant shook hands vigorously and nodded to the chair next to his desk. "Could I get you a cup of coffee? How do you take yours, sir?" He accepted me as if I were an old buddy in whose presence he took the keenest delight, and I mentally kicked my own butt for wasting all that money on phony documentation. Around me, at two dozen identical olive drab desks under the high fluorescent-lit ceiling, the routine busywork of a cop station went on. Reports were laboriously typed on wheezy machines, witnesses were interviewed, mug shots studied, bureaucratic memoranda shoved into In trays, other forms yanked from Out trays. Around the vending machines bored-eyed plainclothesmen swapped lies about their sexual performance the night before.

"The Haskell family certainly spares no expense," Domjan remarked as he sipped from a cup of liquid cardboard.

"I'm . . . not quite sure what you mean," I replied cautiously.

"Well, you know. Sending in two lawyers from Saint Louis to wind up the poor girl's affairs."

My effort to swallow surprise was not terribly successful, but since I already decided not to drink any of the foul coffee I didn't choke on the brew. "Urmm—two lawyers?" I echoed.

Now for the first time Domjan was looking at me with something less than naive pleasure. "Sir," he asked, "didn't you come east with another attorney named Jeffrey Haskell? Miss Haskell's half brother?"

I took his cue and made my first totally truthful statement in the dialogue. "I had no idea Mr. Haskell was in town," I confessed. "I—urmm, my office handles—that is, handled Bradford Haskell's personal legal business. Bradford Haskell, you may know, was Ann and Jeffrey Haskell's father and the founder of Haskell's Supermarkets. Jeff is the chief counsel for the family corporation." I tried to study Domjan's face and form a judgment whether I was convincing him without alerting him that I cared a damn what his reaction was. "Obviously," I went on, "with all the confusion this week, two deaths in the family coming so close together and all that, we seem to have, urmm, gotten our wires crossed."

He bought the package. I could almost see him relax and sit a millimeter less tautly in his ancient chair. The cop skepticism was gone from his blue-gray eyes and he was an eager kid again. "Yesterday morning," he said, "Jeffrey Haskell was sitting right where you are now. He may even still be in town. I don't think he mentioned when he planned to fly back."

"You're, urmm, certain the man you saw was Jeff Haskell?"

"His voice isn't easy to forget," Domjan said.

"So you, urmm, had heard his voice before, I gather?"

"He was the person I spoke to Friday afternoon when I called Saint Louis to break the news to the family about Miss Haskell's—accident. He couldn't come in right away because his own father's funeral service was scheduled for Saturday, but he flew in Saturday evening and spoke to me yesterday morning."

"Then I suppose, urmm, that he has already taken care of most of what needs to be done," I muttered as if to myself.

"Probably," Domjan concurred. "I gave him the keys to her apartment so he could inventory her personal property."

Damn! There went my hope of conning him out of the keys and conducting my own search of her place. I decided to take a long chance and venture a few questions that were not strictly in keeping with my identity as Charles B. Blackburn. If I couldn't wangle official sanction for rummaging through the apartment, I might at least harvest some more facts about her death that hadn't appeared in the newspapers.

"You turned over the keys to Miss Haskell's place without any argument, I take it?" I phrased the question with infinite care, like a lawyer opening up a line of cross-examination.

"Naturally." The sergeant nodded, finished the last of what he fondly believed was coffee, frowned rather disapprovingly at my own still brim-full plastic cup. Could it be that this male version of a perfect Ten actually thought the horse juice was drinkable?

"I take it then that in your opinion there was nothing, urmm, suspicious about Miss Haskell's death? Nothing that would make you want to keep control of access to the scene?"

"Mr. Blackburn," Domjan said, "I can assure you as a professional investigator that there wasn't anything questionable about the accident. It was just one of those—those tragedies that can happen to a person who, you know, drinks too much. In fact . . . Well, let me put it this way, sir. Do you happen to like old movies?"

I blinked, wondering where in God's green world this bizarre conversation was headed now. "I enjoy a wholesome picture now and then," I admitted guardedly.

"You like William Holden's pictures? *Golden Boy? Picnic? The Horse Soldiers* with Duke Wayne?"

"Some of them I like very much. I don't think I've seen him in anything since *Network* several years ago."

"That was a good one. . . . Anyway, I'm sort of hipped on golden-age Hollywood movies and movie people. The minute I walked into Miss Haskell's apartment Friday morning and started looking around, the setup reminded me of the way poor Bill Holden died last year. You remember? He was alone and got drunk and fell and hit his head and died. I tell you, Mr. Blackburn, solitary drinking is dangerous. I don't use alcohol at all myself.

Ahhh . . . Mind if I drink your coffee?" He reached out for my cup and began sipping from it with every sign of relish.

Now was the time to lob the first big question, for the opportunity to ask which I had shelled out three thousand crustaceans. "Are you absolutely certain that—that Miss Haskell was drunk when she—when she had her accident?"

"I'll be happy to show you the medical examiner's report." He leafed through the stack of manila folders aligned with the corner of his desk, pulled the one he was looking for. Turned back a bunch of pages on the metal doodad glued to the upper edge until a particular sheet was topmost. He passed it to me and I scanned verbiage.

"That report shows that there was more than double the volume of alcohol in her blood than what you need in this state to be legally drunk," Domjan explained. "And there was confirmation in her apartment. Her liquor cabinet contained four full quarts of Wild Turkey bourbon, two of Johnnie Walker Red, a bottle of brandy, and an assortment of liqueurs, and there were two empty bourbon bottles in her wastebasket. Her fingerprints were on all of them too."

That was when another of those implosions that blew everything into place went off in my skull, and if Domjan's assurances had raised even a sliver of doubt, suddenly all doubts were blown away as if by a tornado and I was more certain than ever that she'd been murdered. One: *In all the times that she and I had had a drink together, never once had she drunk hard liquor.* As an aperitif she favored sherry on rocks or Chablis, and when we had dinner out we would often share a carafe of wine with the main course. Afterward, brandy or one of her well-beloved liqueurs. Two: *None of those quarts of Wild Turkey and Johnnie Red had been in her liquor cabinet as of four in the morning a week ago Saturday.* But if she hadn't bought them and put them with her own supply, then someone else had, and had put her fingerprints on the bottles too. And I had to sit there in the straight-backed chair and keep my mouth shut and carry on my role as Blackburn the Saint Louis lawyer, while the things I knew and Domjan didn't were eating my insides like corrosive acids.

"Sad," I clucked in simulation of abstract sympathy. "I suppose you must be right, Sergeant, and after all I'm no detective. But of course there is a difference between Miss Haskell's death—or at least, the circumstances of her death as the New York papers reported them—and the death of William Holden. If I recall correctly, Mr. Holden's body wasn't found until several days after he died. But Miss Haskell's was discovered the very morning after the, urmm, tragedy."

Sometimes the best way to get the answer you want is not to ask the question but just to skirt around its border. If the strategy didn't work on Domjan I made up my mind to ask point blank. The luck was with me that morning.

"An anonymous phone call came into the precinct reporting an accident in that apartment," the underage sergeant volunteered. "The call was logged in at . . . " He tugged the file out of my hand, flipped pages. "Right, at eight oh three A.M. Just after I'd come on duty. I had the eight-to-four shift last week, the same as I do now."

"You don't know who it was that called in the report?"

"No idea. That kind of thing happens all the time. Neighbor who doesn't want to get involved."

"You took the call yourself?"

"No. One of the desk sergeants."

"Then you can't say whether it was a man's voice or a woman's?"

He hunted through pages in the file folder again.

"Desk sergeant stated that he thought it was a man's. Mr. Blackburn, I really don't understand all these questions. There's no doubt at all about how Miss Haskell died."

Ah, you poor innocent child of a cop, if only you knew how true that statement was! But I sensed that Domjan wasn't going to tolerate further pumping. I could get away with one more question, maybe, but it had damn well better be something worth asking. How about: When you searched the apartment, did you happen to find a will? No. Not worth the risk. With no evidence of anything suspicious, they wouldn't have been looking for anything except the address and phone number of her next of kin so they could be notified. And anyway even if she kept a will in the apartment, which was wildly unlikely in view of her real identity, Jeffrey Haskell must have located it by now. How about: Has any private detective dropped in since her death and reported that he'd been hired by Jeff Haskell to shadow his alleged half sister? No, that wasn't worth blowing my cover for either. If there had been a snoop on her trail and he'd told the cops after the accident that Jeffrey Haskell had had doubts about Ann's identity and hired him to check her out, Domjan wouldn't have blithely turned over to Jeffrey the keys to Ann's apartment. Which could mean either that Jeff was bluffing and never did retain a peeper or that Mr. Peeper hadn't come to the cops after his quarry's sudden death.

I gave up. Anything else I was going to learn would have to be learned outside the police station. I toyed with the handle of my attaché case and made body signals indicating that I was about to buzz off.

But before I could lift myself out of the chair, Sergeant Domjan casually dropped the bomb on me.

"You must be concerned about the effect of Miss

Haskell's death on her share of her father's estate," he said.

"Well, to a certain extent," I replied automatically. "But once her will is found, assuming of course that she left a will—"

"Oh, but Mr. Blackburn," the kid sergeant pointed out brightly, "even if she did leave a will, wouldn't the hundred-twenty-hour rule cut her off and keep Bradford Haskell's property from passing under her will?" He favored me with a broad grin as if we were both members of the same lodge and tapped the pile of thousand-page tomes at the far corner of his desk. From the titles on the spines I saw that they were law school casebooks. "I take night courses at Fordham Law," he said. "In fact, my exam in Estates and Administration was just last week, so I'm pretty well up on the hundred-twenty-hour rule."

"Oh, yes. Of course. Naturally," I chimed in as if I fully comprehended what Domjan was blabbering about. "Hundred-twenty-hour rule, that's right." I thanked the sergeant for his valuable time and shook his strong young hand and strode lawyerlike out of the detective division, passing in my march down to the street an array of cops in uniform and cops in suits, cops white and black and brown and male and female who, such is the blessed diversity of the American people, had only one thing in common besides their job. None of them paid me the least attention on my way out of their bailiwick.

The May morning was too beautiful to be wasted in a taxi and I decided to walk it back to Central Park South. Madison was packed with men and women on the move, some headed north and some south, some in jaunty suits or bright spring dresses, others in blue jeans and ragged tops. On any other day of the sort I would have kept an eye cocked for the visions of bodily grace who are always to be seen on the main drags of the city. Not today. The Milonic brain was whirling and tumbling like a prisoner inside a hyperactive laundry dryer. What the hell had Sergeant Beefcake meant by the hundred-twenty-hour rule? Was he right that even though Ann Haskell had demonstrably outlived her father she couldn't take the third of his residuary that his will had left her, and therefore couldn't pass her property on in any will of her own? Then maybe, just maybe, the Jock's common sense notion of estate law was dead off the mark, and either of the Haskell brothers who knew this hundred-twenty-hour gimmick would have had a magnificent motive to kill Ann even after Bradford Haskell's death.

I had to find someone who could tutor me in the legal principles I needed to know, and on my way west along Central Park South I worked out that part of the plan. But it could keep till tomorrow. I stopped at the condo just long enough to use the john and shed the artifacts of my Charles Blackburn identity. Then I went out again into the morning, back the way I'd gone before.

To her place.

I pressed the entranceway buzzer to her apartment and was greeted by stone silence. Jeffrey had been through her possessions and long since flown back to Missouri. If I had found him pawing over her clothes and papers I think I would have killed him on the spot. I beat the street-door lock with a credit card and the lock on the front door of her apartment with Handy Dandy the skeleton key.

First I ran a superficial search of the place, hands in pockets, draping a paper towel from the kitchen roll over my fingers whenever I had to touch a knob or a drawer handle. All the furniture was where I remembered it should be. The throw rug she was supposed to have slipped on was aligned with the fake fireplace as if no foot had ever trod its surface. I tried not to look at the blood smear that had darkened the parquet. The cabinet with the sliding door held all the booze Domjan had mentioned: four quarts of Wild Turkey and two of Johnnie Red up front, the brandy and liqueurs in a second row behind the hard liquor. Rearranged radically and augmented substantially from the way it had been a week ago Saturday morning.

Her clothes still hung neatly in the closets or were folded fastidiously in the dresser drawers, her perfumes still waited for her on the bureau top. But the kidney-shaped desk in the living room was bare of papers. Whatever documentation she had glommed from the San Francisco apartment of the one and only original Ann Haskell soon after that lady's accident had now been glommed by her half brother soon after the accident—only it wasn't an accident—to her replacement. The weird patterns life makes.

I sat on the couch and shut my eyes and tried to say good-bye to her, tried to let her go. The apartment was dead quiet and the building was dead quiet, a cocoon inside a cocoon. The silence fed my sense of guilt. The first time we had been together in this city, I had done something stupid and she had paid for it by having two fingers broken with a hammer. The second time we were together here, I was having a goddamn dream about making love to her while she was being brutalized and murdered. As I sat there on her couch I could almost see it happening, the way it must have been. Sneak quietly into the apartment with a gun and eight bottles of liquor. Get the drop on her and force her to pour the better part of two quarts of bourbon down her throat. Watch her shake in terror and beg for her life and try with everything she had to fight the effect of the booze. Did it gag her? Make her vomit? Any mess was cleaned up afterward with professional skill. Then when she's so drunk she's beyond caring what happens to her anymore, they kill her. Knock her head in and arrange the details of the accident, modeled on the death of William Holden. Movie buffs.

I have no idea how long I sat there working through the new wave of insight and grief and guilt. Finally I knew it was time to go. I took a last look around the apartment, not for more evidence but as a sort of good-bye ritual, knowing I'd never be this close to her again.

In her bedroom, very faint but just perceptible enough to hit me low and make me cry out, I still caught the scent of her.

TEN

Law! The vision of a world encased in rules, gasping for breath amid the python coils of statutes, judicial decisions, administrative regulations, executive orders, every single directive requiring a cadre of lawyers to codify and clarify and interpret and argue and expound for the nonlawyer public. Towards this ultimate goal the legal profession strives. Law is the national narcotic and someday we will overdose on it and die.

Taken in moderation, it stimulates me.

From the notebooks of Milo Turner

Tuesday morning, with the mercury at sixty and the sky sea blue above the building tops, I cabbed downtown to West Fourth Street in the heart of Greenwich Village, my destination a red brick edifice labeled Vanderbilt Hall, which is the home of New York University School of Law. The receptionist in the dean's complex glanced at my press credentials and informed me that Estates and Administration was being taught this semester by a visiting professor named Mensing. She buzzed his office on the third floor and announced that he'd be happy to talk with me and pointed in the direction of the elevator.

He was waiting in the corridor when I stepped out of the cage, a big bearish fellow with thick glasses that made him look like a pro football quarterback with myopia. "Loren Mensing," he introduced himself with extended hand. "I've been interviewed by a lot of newspapers but never by *Time* before. My office is cluttered with examination papers. Mind if we talk in the faculty library?"

He led the way to a high-ceilinged chamber bright with fluorescent light, a place for soft scholarly voices and calm reflection, with bound volumes of law journals filling shelves along all four walls. We poured coffee from a silver urn near the fireplace and crossed the dark blue carpet to a pair of easy chairs in an alcove. He was hopelessly taken in by the paper and plastic that identified me as a Mr. Garrett from *Time* magazine, a persona which I keep on permanent standby for use when I need information. I was a member of the team assigned to a major piece on what happens to people's money after they die, and he had been suggested as a resource person. He was only too eager to help. After a decent interval for coffee-sipping and chatter I raised the subject I'd come here to pick his brains on.

"I'm not a lawyer, of course, but I've been learning some fascinating things about law on this assignment. For example, someone was telling me just the other day that if a person leaves me property in his will, even if I outlive the person I can still lose the bequest. Something about a hundred-twenty-hour rule . . . "

"Right." Mensing picked up the thread just where I had carefully allowed it to trail off. "It's a rule under the Uniform Probate Code, which more and more states are adopting."

"Could you explain how it works? I'm still confused by the whole thing." I bent to my spiral notebook like the epitome of a conscientious journalist.

"Okay. Suppose several members of the same family are in an accident and die within a few days of each other. The hundred-twenty-hour rule will . . . Excuse me, let me grab a book that will help me explain." He trotted to a shelf and brought back a green-bound volume with *Uniform Laws Annotated* on its spine and hunted for a page.

"Here it is. Section 2–601 of the Uniform Probate Code says in essence that unless the testator's will provides otherwise, any legatee who dies within one hundred twenty hours *after* the testator is treated as if he'd died *before* the testator. The purpose of the statute is to avoid multiple probate proceedings and multiple estate taxation on the same property."

"Let me make sure I understand," I cut in politely. "Say Mr. Jones has a will that leaves the residue of his estate to Smith and Brown in equal shares." I constructed the hypothetical situation as I went along, trying my damnedest to parallel the facts in the Haskell case without giving away my interest in anything beyond the abstract rule itself. Jones equaled Bradford Haskell, Smith stood for Ann (the real daughter or the fake), and Brown played a dual role as the old man's sons by his second marriage. "Jones died, oh, say two days ago. Smith drops dead today." Which was just about the interval between Bradford Haskell's death and my lady's. "If I understand the hundred-twenty-hour rule, Smith's death so close to Mr. Jones's death sort of disqualifies him as a taker under Jones's will, and all of Mr. Jones's estate goes to Brown." And Brown, meaning either or both of the Haskell brothers, would have had one sixth of ten million dollars' worth of motive apiece to kill Smith—meaning the woman they took for their half sister—within one hundred twenty hours of their father's death. "Right?" While I waited for confirmation from Mensing my mind ran ahead of reality, toying with modes of vengeance, grappling with the question of which of the brothers was guilty, tempted by the obvious suggestion that I should hire a hit man to waste them both.

"Not necessarily." Mensing's negative headshake jolted me back to the here and now of the cool law faculty library.

I couldn't believe what he was telling me. "Where did I go wrong?" I demanded of him, fighting to keep frustration out of my voice.

"Well, you just haven't given me enough facts in your hypothetical so that I can give you the result. Depending on the family situation of the people, the hundred-twenty-hour rule could be overridden by the antilapse statute."

I must have stared at him slack-jawed like a cretin, because the next moment he sprang out of the easy chair and began pacing the worn blue carpet like a caged tiger—or a prof in a classroom. "Remember," he began, "all that Section 2–601 says is that if Smith dies within one hundred twenty hours after Jones, he's treated as if he died before Jones did. Now, if we were still under the common law, your conclusion would be correct. Smith would take nothing from Mr. Jones's estate, Smith's will wouldn't pass anything from Jones's estate to Smith's own legatees, and all of Jones's property would go to Brown. This is because in common law, when a legatee died before the testator, the bequest to that legatee was held to *lapse*—in other words to be null and void. Follow me so far?"

"I think so," I muttered, scrawling frantically in my notebook.

"But," he went on with the excitement of the born lecturer animating his voice and gestures, "the Uniform Code and the codes of most states now have so-called antilapse statutes. The purpose of an antilapse statute is to save *some* lapsed bequests for the benefit of the predeceased person's direct descendants, provided two conditions are met. First, that the predeceased legatee has one or more descendants, and second, that the relationship between the predeceased legatee and the testator falls within the protected degree of closeness."

That was an excess of legalese for my poor layman's head. I looked up from my notes like a puppy begging for a soupbone. "Please," I said, "may I have a concrete example of what you're talking about?"

"Glad to." Mensing flipped a few pages forward in the green-bound lawbook. "The Uniform Code's antilapse statute is Section 2–605. Let's use the names in your example again. If Smith was Mr. Jones's grandparent, or his parent, or his child, or his grandchild, then he falls within the protected degree of closeness in relationship to Jones. Now, if Smith satisfies that condition, *and* if Smith left descendants of his or her own who survive Mr. Jones by one hundred twenty hours, then the antilapse statute—well, let's say it bumps the hundred-twenty-hour rule that would otherwise disqualify Smith, and the result is that Smith's descendants take in his or her place what would have been Smith's share of Mr. Jones's estate." He paused for breath, stopped pacing, dropped back into the easy chair across from me. "Got it?"

Boom! Implosion. Satori. Things came together again in harmony, and in one blinding moment I saw precisely how I would avenge my woman's murder. I struggled to keep a poker face—not that Professor Four Eyes could have seen the expectancy spreading over me—and, just to make sure I didn't misunderstand, probed a few feet deeper into the bowels of the law.

"I'm not sure if I have it clear or not. Would it be all right if I tried a few more hypothetical situations on you?"

"Be my guest." Mensing sat back in the armchair and folded his hands atop a crossed knee.

"Let's suppose," I postulated, "that Mr. Jones's will leaves the residue of his estate in equal shares to—make it his son Andy and his daughter Candy." With Andy again standing in for the pair of Haskell sons, and Candy representing the daughter, or my dead lady. "Mr. Jones died two days ago. Candy drops dead today, or anytime within one hundred twenty hours after her father's death. Now, let me see if I have this right. If Candy has no child of her own, then Andy winds up with the entire residue of Mr. Jones's estate. Right?"

Mensing nodded, beckoning me with his hands, seeming to want to pull the answers out of me with his gestures, urging me on.

"But," I continued, fever-voiced, "if Candy *did* have a child or children of her own, then the kid or kids take what would have been Candy's half share of the residue of old Mr. Jones's estate?"

"Exactly. Just as the children would if Candy had actually died before Mr. Jones." Mensing's voice rang with the pride of a professor who had finally penetrated the mind of an idiot student.

"And this is the law in all fifty states?"

"Again, not necessarily." Mensing held up his palm like a crossing guard halting the flow of traffic. "The details vary in each jurisdiction."

Another goddamn roadblock! Before I committed myself to my script for revenge I had to be sure that the hundred-twenty-hour rule and the antilapse statute as I now understood them were the law in Missouri, the state whose probate code governed the disposition of Bradford Haskell's property. But I couldn't afford to let slip that I had any particular curiosity about the jurisprudence of the Show-Me State.

In as close as I could approximate the tone of a bored wage slave doing the dull job he was paid for, I inquired about the status of these rules in New York and a few other states whose legislation left me cold. Obliging as ever—God, how he must have craved a long break from those examinations he'd been grading!—Mensing hunted through tomes on the faculty library shelves and treated me to brief lectures on each state's variations. Fifth on my list was Missouri, and I held my breath as he thumbed through a volume of *Vernon's Annotated Missouri Statutes.*

"Missouri's rules are essentially the same," he announced, snapping the book shut. "Both its hundred-twenty-hour rule and its antilapse statute are modeled more or less on the Uniform Code provisions."

"Let's try Iowa," I suggested for good measure.

Ten minutes later I pocketed my bulging notebook and unchaired myself and stretched and retraced my steps through the third-floor corridors of the law school with my bearlike guide through the labyrinth at my side and my mind light-years away. At the elevator Mensing pressed the button for me and I shook hands with him in boundless gratitude. "Professor," I told him with absolute honesty, "you've been a fantastic help."

"Always happy to spread knowledge of the law." He smiled, and the cage door sliced us apart.

The balance of Tuesday I spent buttoned up in my high-rise cave, oblivious to the beauties of the day, too preoccupied even to twirl the radio dial and find background music. Like the hypothetical Mr. Brown in the problem I had posed in the NYU law faculty library, I was performing a dual role. First I was the great detective. Not Arthur Lattman, the in-again-out-again private eye whose mythical exploits dazzled the gullible, but more of a Sherlock Holmes or Ellery Queen figure, the walking intellect who pieces together all the little clues that point like arrows to the truth. Simultaneously I was the chess master, the Clausewitz of crime with a genius for fashioning the strategic gambit that would cream the opposition. My approach bore a cousinly resemblance to the way a Beethoven might take a few musical ideas caught in a burst of intuition and develop them into a formally intricate and emotionally stunning work like the Ninth Symphony. By the time the sun sank behind the Jersey Palisades the plan had assumed for me an abstract beauty very much like an orchestral piece, or the choreography for a magnificent ballet. The long day's labor left me wiped out and more awed than ever at the world's musical giants.

It was time to try out a few of my ideas on the life's foremost aesthetic critic, to whom as it happened I also owed an apology. The explanation would be lengthy, and I didn't want the call billed to George Boyd's number, nor did I relish the prospect of standing in the open before a public phone for an hour or more. I tapped out the special access code that would instruct Ma Bell's computer to charge the call to the third wealthiest corporation in the United States, then touched the digits that brought me the voice of the Jock.

"Me again," I said. "I have a pile of news for you, Jocko, but first I have to tell you how sorry I am. I had no right to scream at you that way the last time."

"Ahhh, forget it, lad! It was the grief bad-mouthing me, not the man. Ye think I have not known grief?"

"I've made up my mind about one thing," I told him. "I'll never get involved with another woman the way I did with her. It—hurts so goddamn *deep,* Jocko."

"We wouldn't be Irish if we didn't know that someday the world would break our hearts," he said softly. Then, forcing me to concentrate on something I could handle better, he changed the subject. "But ye say ye have news for me too. What is it, me buck?"

"It involves a lot of legal jargon and detective work but the bottom line is that she was murdered and I know who was behind it." I recapped my visit to the cop house and Sergeant Domjan's account of the accident scene and the hundred-twenty-hour bombshell he had dropped and my own good-bye look at her apartment and my morning's visit in the guise of a *Time* researcher to the lair of Professor Mensing. The Jock caught the implication of the hundred-twenty-hour rule as quickly as I had myself, and proved it during a lull while I was irrigating the tonsils with Dewar's.

"So common sense and mother wit played me false," he said. "It's not enough for a person who's been left property in a will just to outlive the person who wrote the will, he has to survive the fellow by one hundred twenty hours."

"In most states that seems to be the law," I agreed.

"I wouldn't call it the best-known rule of law in the world, would ye now?"

"I doubt if more than a handful of nonlawyers have ever heard of it."

"So," he said with an almost audible mental smack of the lips. "That's what tells ye which brother is the murderer?"

"It sure helps. Jeffrey, the head of Haskell's Supermarkets legal department, is much more likely to have known he could enrich himself by the difference between a third and a half of ten mil by killing the woman he assumed was his half sister. And even his father's sudden death didn't make it too late for him."

"Ye might say, though, that Bradford Haskell's death started the running of the clock."

"Right. A clock that ran for one hundred twenty hours. If Ann died within that deadline Jeff would still take an extra million and two thirds."

"Ah, but mightn't ye be overlooking something?" the Jock suggested insidiously.

"God, I hope not. I'm strung out from running it through my head since noon. What have I left out?"

"Well, it strikes the old Jock that ye have at least three possible murderers to contend with: Jeffrey alone, Eugene the symphony violinist alone, and the two of them, if ye'll forgive me, in concert. So far ye've gone a long way towards ruling out young Gene alone. But couldn't the brothers have done it together? After all, Ann's dying when she did added more than a million six hundred thousand to each of the brother's shares. And ye don't want to neglect the other possibilities either."

"Jock, I don't believe for one minute that either or both of them came here and killed her in person, if that's what you're driving at. First, it would have been too risky, second, I don't think either of them could get away to New York right after the old man's funeral without being missed, and third, the killing was too professional. Jeff bought a hit man." Just like the fat pol in North Jersey had thought he was buying me.

"A very special hit man he must have found," the Jock said. "One who combined knowledge, imagination, and speed."

"He brought those eight quarts of booze with him to her place. Made her drink at gunpoint till there was a huge amount of alcohol in her blood. Then he—he killed her and made it look like the way William Holden died last year. But remember, Holden's body wasn't found for days afterward. Our man had to make sure there was no doubt that she died while the hundred-twenty-hour clock was still ticking. So around eight the next morning he made that anonymous call to the cops, reporting an accident in her apartment."

Jock picked up the reconstruction. "And the police find the poor girl's body, and notify her half brothers."

"Then a few hours after his father's buried, Jeffrey wings into town and the cops give him the keys to her place and he cleans out all her papers, which of course the hit man couldn't do himself because their absence might have suggested murder and robbery."

"Ye keep insisting it was Jeffrey, don't ye, lad? Well, I'm convinced she was murdered, but I've yet to have it shown to me satisfaction that Jeffrey was responsible."

"Still think it might have been the two of them together, eh? Jocko, if you look at the timing you'll see that the conspiracy theory won't wash. Look, as a lawyer Jeffrey knows that the hundred-twenty-hour clock will start ticking as soon as his father kicks off. The old man has had several heart attacks. He might die in a few hours or he might last for years. Right?"

"The human heart is a most unpredictable organ," he murmured.

"But remember, until a few weeks ago, when Ann made herself and her whereabouts known to the family by visiting them in Saint Louis, Jeffrey *had no idea his half sister would pop into the picture*! Before then he couldn't have known if she were dead or alive, rich in her own right or starving somewhere as a bag lady. Until she showed up there's no way she could have figured in his calculations. Agreed?"

"I won't argue the point with ye."

"But don't you see? It's ridiculous to think he could have worked out his scheme, found the right hit man, and put the guy on standby alert in that short a time! Not totally impossible, but damn implausible. It's a hell of a lot more likely that he'd started his scheme *before* Ann showed up. Now, is there someone else whose 'accidental' death within a hundred twenty hours of his father's death would benefit Jeffrey? You bet your ass there is. *His brother Gene.*"

"Ahhh," the Jock sighed comprehension. "So ye postulate that his original plan was to kill his brother, either before his father died or within one hundred twenty hours afterward. And—this is before he knew about the half sister of course—the entire ten million dollars in his father's residuary estate would pass to him under the will."

"Even if he did think of Ann and assumed she'd take a third, his share would still go from a third to a half," I pointed out.

"So when Ann—or rather, the lady he took for Ann entered the picture, he switched the target from his brother to her?"

"Right! She lived a thousand miles away, he had no emotional ties to her, there was less risk that the cops would connect the two deaths. All sorts of reasons for . . . " Suddenly I caught an aspect that I'd missed or hadn't let myself see before, and it hit me like a knife thrust in the belly. "Oh Jesus, Jock. She—thought she was so close to collecting that money and retiring from the life, and all the time she was walking into a booby trap and saving the guy that was originally intended to take the hit."

"We all walk a bit closer to death every day, lad," the Jock reminded me softly. Then, deflecting me again to something I could manage, "But exactly how do ye propose to respond, boy? Tell the old fool what marvel ye've spent the day devising."

"Is the supermarket open?"

"We never close when a friend is hungry. What do ye need?"

"A child," I told him.

"A *what*?" The Schultzian exclamation combined incredulity and indignation and a hint that in his considered opinion I had gone bananas.

"A white child," I specified. "Age four or five. Doesn't matter if it's a boy or a girl, but the kid should look a tad like me if possible. And a woman, of course, to take care of the child. A gal who can cope with trouble."

"A woman and child," he repeated. "And must they come as a package, or will ye settle for a lady who is not the tyke's mother?"

"It would help a bunch if she was," I said.

"I'll work on it," he promised. "Now, what else do ye need for the mission?"

"The rest I can buy from Lafferty. Certain documents have to be forged and placed in the right public records. That's the part that will take time. And I'll need new identities for three people, but Lafferty can do that."

The line was silent for about thirty seconds of Jockian pondering, then his lilt came back. "It's an expensive campaign ye seem to be mounting. I estimate a hundred thousand minimum, which ye'll never recover."

"I don't give a damn if it costs every cent I've put away. This isn't a money-making operation."

"And ye don't care to say how the divil ye plan to use these human props?"

"I'm still fiddling with the details. But the gist of it is that I'm going to put a show together and take it on the road."

"To what destination, may the old fool inquire?"

"To Saint Louis," I said.

ELEVEN

What is it that the great movie directors do? Critics have spilled gallons of ink debating that question, but the best answer is simplicity itself. The great director, like the great creator in any other field, makes a world distinctively his own. There is nothing quite like the El Greco look, or the Bartók sound, or the Faulkner sentence. The suspense classics of Hitchcock, the comedies of Capra, the visually explosive actionfests of that unsung titan William Witney—each is a distinguishable universe enticing us to enter and participate. Creating such a universe is the great director's business.

And mine.

From the notebooks of Milo Turner

Setting the stage took six weeks of dog labor, while New York sweltered through a late spring heat wave. I lived most of that time as a hermit. With the air conditioner turned up to full blast I spent hours each day asprawl in my recliner armchair, hacking my way through jungles of legalese verbiage. The annotated paperback edition of the Uniform Probate Code. Averill's *Uniform Probate Code in a Nutshell.* The multivolume treatise known as *Page on Wills.* I was determined never again to be ambushed by technicalities of the law during this operation. When I couldn't bear another paragraph of heavy-footed analysis I took a break and made some of the phone calls or prepared some of the paperwork to close out a few of my retirement accounts in certain banks.

Evenings consisted of a scratch meal and a subway ride to the Village and a long session with Lafferty on the pile of fake documents I'd commissioned. When one set of papers was completed to my satisfaction I'd have to hit the phone again, calling various connections around the country, making arrangements to get the documents notarized and certified and inserted in the proper depository of public records.

For support troops I tapped into Jock's supermart yet again, and that miracle man from the Emerald Isle never failed me. One might say to him, as I said a few weeks into the preparations, "Jocko, I need a Saint Louis lawyer. A solo practitioner, not part of a big assembly-line firm. He has to know the law of wills and estates the way he knows his ABCs. I want someone who's a tiger at the bargaining table and a pussycat when it comes to believing his client's lies. And he has to be desperate for a big case. What can you do for me?" The Jock would ask me to call him back in forty-eight hours, and upon my doing so he might say, as he did to me, "Mr. David Keel is the lawyer ye seek. He has an office in Clayton, which is the seat of Saint Louis County and just west of the city proper. A man in his middle thirties with ten years' experience mainly in the field of estates, but all bread-and-butter work, nothing sizable in the planning line or litigation. A man very sensitive about his prematurely bald pate. He wears an expensive rug that doesn't fit his head right. He's married and leads a quiet private life. Outside his practice the man's a fool." The next morning I called Mr. Keel person-to-person, sounded him out, described a somewhat hypothetical situation briefly and vaguely and without mentioning my name or any other, and upon eliciting his curiosity I promised I'd be in touch with him again.

Further along in the planning stages I called the Jock for another side of beef from his market. "It's the bodyguard detail," I explained. "What's the most reliable security outfit in Saint Louis that won't investigate the client too closely?"

"That answer I can give ye without making ye wait. Eagle Eye Investigations, located in the Parkway Building in downtown Saint Louis. It's owned by Luther Zwack. Did ye know him when he was in the life?"

"Nope. Heard of him, though. Didn't he change careers and become a private peeper about fifteen years back?"

"He's the one. A strange bird he is, but sound. Ye can trust him with what ye're about if ye've a mind to."

"I'll think about it. Er, have you had any luck getting me that child we talked about? I know a special order like that will take time. . . . "

"Do ye think so?" Jock chuckled softly. "Then take down this address, laddie. Twenty–twenty-five Twenty-ninth Street. That's in Astoria, only a short hop by subway from where ye live. A private house whose top floor is rented by one Suzanne French, a competent but unknown artist. She is comely to look upon, perpetually short of cash, and the proud mither of a daughter aged four. In the parlance of the great American sport, lad, I call that a triple play."

"Jock," I said, "without you I would have slit my throat years ago."

That evening, when I looked up her number in the book and called to ask for an appointment, she said in a cool guarded telephone voice that she'd see me at noon and gave me directions.

The BMT train marked RR takes about twenty minutes to jounce its patrons from the Fifty-ninth Street station to the end of the line at Ditmars Boulevard in the Astoria section of Queens. I climbed down from the elevated platform into what could have passed for a street scene in Athens. The sky stretched milk-blue overhead, unbroken by a single high rise. Greek lettering on most of the shop signs. Sidewalks full of people chattering in native tongues. Smells of spanakopita and pastizio, souvlaki and heavenly baklava. Following her directions I strolled up Thirty-first Street, swung left at Ditmars, took a right at Twenty-ninth and then north up a gentle slope past neat two-story houses, their flat roofs concealed by a facade of steep sloping shingles. Ahead of me the jets from LaGuardia roared out of sight into the blue. The high noon church bells exploded around the neighborhood like a blast from a quad stereo system.

I turned in at a modest brick building with 20–25 in dulled gold-flake figures on a porch column, climbed front steps, and pressed the upper buzzer in the door frame, the one with S. FRENCH beside it. She didn't keep me waiting in the sun cookery. I heard steps on stairs, the front door opened and there she stood.

"Mr. Blake?" She was a trim and delectable lady, five and a half feet tall, with dancing hazel eyes and soft auburn hair curling past the neck of her faded smock to her shoulder blades. I put her age at twenty-six. "I'm Suzy French." The hand she extended was delicate but strong. "Please come upstairs." I followed her up the narrow carpeted flight.

At the head of the stairs I stopped and let my eyes wander. Most of this second floor was a single spacious room. One corner with a flower-patterned armchair and love seat and a simple pressboard coffee table made up the living room. A round maple dining table and four matching curve-backed chairs were placed near the open doorway to the kitchen. The rest of the room was studio. Sunlight poured down through a bubble window in the roof, palettes and brushes and paint tubes and cleaning fluids cluttered a battered tabletop, canvases leaned at angles against white-painted walls hung with bright art-museum posters and framed paintings that I assumed were her own.

"Sorry for the mess," she said. "Artists are notoriously sloppy housekeepers."

"You keep the clutter confined to the studio," I complimented her. "That's more than a lot of creative people do."

"Let's sit and talk." She motioned me to the bargain-basement love seat, detoured into the kitchen and came back with a silex pot of coffee in one hand and two mugs in garish Toulouse-Lautrec colors dangling by their handles from the fingers of the other. She set the paraphernalia on the pressboard table, stripped off the smock to reveal a loose tan blouse and blue jeans, dropped into the armchair. "So you're interested in commissioning some paintings, Mr. Blake?"

"I might very well be. But first, if I could just see some of your work . . . "

She jackknifed out of the chair and trotted to the studio area and came back with a leather portfolio three feet square, unzipped it and displayed what it held. Neighborhood scenes, including a church I'd passed on my way here. Faces of ancient Greek immigrants, group studies of kids cavorting in a schoolyard. Several portraits of the same child, a tiny sweet-faced girl with pale blond hair and café au lait eyes that looked out at the world eagerly and curiously and without a trace of awe or fright. I knew who the child must be but kept to my show of ignorance, and nonchalantly compared her face with her mother's. Very little resemblance. That was a point in her favor.

"Lovely little girl," I said. "Does she live in the neighborhood?"

"My daughter," Suzanne French said proudly.

"The way you paint her shows how much you love her. It comes through in your other work too."

"My loving Joanne?" She wasn't sure what I meant.

"An openness." I tried to pin it down with more specific words. "A givingness. I'm not sure how to say it. The quality I can never feel in abstract art. A commitment to reality, maybe? Anyway, I like your work very much and I do want to give you a commission, if you have the time."

"Mr. Blake, I'm not a rich woman and I have a child to raise. I have the time if you have the money."

So we hunkered down and talked business. It was a ticklish negotiation. She knew her own financial needs and had a healthy respect for her own artistic talent, but if she set her price too high I might take my commission and find someone cheaper. I saw that she was playing it that way and tried to live up to my assigned part. But what I knew and she didn't was that as long as her price was halfway reasonable I was going to retain her. I liked her looks, her emotional instincts, her artist's vision. On canvas at least, I liked her child. It was unlikely I'd find such a package elsewhere. So I let her propose a price she thought was the upper limit of what I was ready to pay, and then I told her she was undervaluing herself and offered a figure of fifteen percent higher for each painting she completed for me, with the proviso that either of us could halt the arrangement if dissatisfied with the other.

"Done," she said, and offered her hand again.

"Now let's seal the bargain by my taking you to lunch," I suggested.

"I'd love to," she said, "but my daughter's sleeping in the bedroom and I really can't leave her alone that long."

"The invitation was for the whole family," I said.

"Then I accept for both of us." She smiled. "Will you excuse me while I wake Joanne up and tell her the good news? There's wine in the fridge, if you don't mind

Almadén from the corner store." She jackknifed out of the chair again and headed for a closed door at the far end of the studio.

Fifteen minutes later they emerged in tandem. The child's head came up to the midpoint of her mother's thighs. Her cornflower-blue hair ribbon matched her dress, and she walked like an artist's model, with pride in her little body. "Mr. Blake," Suzy said, "this is my daughter Joanne."

"Good afternoon, Mr. Blake," she said in a high grave voice, and stuck out her hand, dignified as a society hostess. "I'm very pleased to make your acquaintance. Is Mother going to paint your portrait?"

It was all I could do to repress a double take. This four-year-old had the vocabulary and fluency of early adolescence and the dignity of a mature adult. Her mother giggled mildly at my astonishment and threw her arm around the girl's shoulder.

"Everybody reacts to Joanne that way," she said. "But after all, the only reason little children talk what we think of as baby talk is because that's how their parents talk to them. Even when Joanne was an infant I never went *goo-goo* and *maa-maa* to her. On her first birthday I took her all over the apartment and told her the name of everything she saw. 'This is the kitchen. This is the stove. This is the bedroom. This is the love seat.' If you don't talk down to children but treat them like adults they'll respond the same way."

"Wow," I said inanely. "Did you ever think of just painting for fun and going into the parental counseling business?"

We walked to a luncheonette a few blocks away, a mom-and-pop enterprise with checkered tablecloths and soda-fountain chairs and a long mural of Piraeus on the wall, and ordered gyros—sandwiches on pita bread—with Greek salad on the side. Joanne settled for a cup of lemon soup and a few bites of her mother's sandwich and then a couple from mine as well, topped off with the part of the meal she was really waiting for, an ice cream cone. She nibbled quietly while Suzy and I talked art, a subject of which my ignorance is abysmal. I volunteered nothing about why I was commissioning the paintings and she said no more about her personal life. But a few casual comments hinted strongly to me that she and the child were alone in the world, which as far as I was concerned was not only desirable but a necessity. I wrote her a check for three hundred dollars before we said good-bye outside the restaurant and I strolled back through sun heat and street crowds to the elevated subway stop at Ditmars.

We began work the next morning. "An apartment in the East Fifties," I said, and handed her a rough sketch I'd made on the back of a piece of George Boyd's junk mail. "Living room, kitchenette, bedroom. Parquet floor. There's a fake fireplace along this wall with a, you know, a throw rug in front of it. This is a liquor cabinet here. I want the sliding door pushed back so the bottles show. No hard stuff," I said too loudly. "Just brandy and liqueurs. You can go to a package store and paint in whatever bottles catch your eye."

First she did rough charcoal sketches, each one more detailed and vivid than the last, until the layout was right. Then we talked about colors, perspective, angles of vision. I told her to do one painting as if the spectator were sitting in the kitchenette, another from the living room couch, a third from the bedroom doorway. What all the canvases had in common was the fake fireplace and the throw rug and the sliding-doored liquor cabinet. I was going to have her do a sketch of the bedroom, but there was too much pain in the memory of the way it was there and I decided not to risk describing it for her in detail. The other paintings were enough. We worked

126

five days a week from nine thirty in the morning till one in the afternoon, while Joanne watched us quiet as a baby bunny or gravely excused herself and vanished into the bedroom to watch TV.

The second week, I described my lady. I am a rotten artist, constitutionally incapable of rendering a human or even an animal on paper. I tried to draw a horse once and it came out looking like a jackrabbit. At first my verbal descriptions were little better, so she asked me questions. The exact shade of her eyes, how she wore her hair, the way she held her hands when she was standing. Like a police artist working with a crime victim to produce a sketch of the perpetrator, she dashed off a sheaf of quick tentative images, and each one came that much closer to my dear woman as I remembered her.

At the start of the third week she went to canvas. I sat in one of the curve-backed dining room chairs and watched the dead come to life under the magic of Suzy's brushes. Her eyes, her mouth, her vibrant body lived again and terrified me, made me want to run and hide. *Why couldn't you save me?* she seemed to say.

"Stop it," I told Suzy. "Please. No more. Don't do any more today. Let's just—break early, okay?"

Her eyes filled with silent understanding of whatever she must have seen in mine. "Sure," she said quietly, and tossed her spattered smock over a vacant easel. "The light's lousy anyway. Coffee? Wine? Want to tell me about her?"

Over the thirteen mornings we had worked together I could sense her holding back the mounting curiosity she was feeling about these paintings. I had had ample time to observe her reactions, take my soundings, psych myself for the next stage of the campaign. Now was the moment for thumbs up or thumbs down. Either I told her the story or I thanked her and waved good-bye and found someone else.

"Wine," I said. "Yes, I think we'd better have a long talk."

We sat at opposite ends of the love seat with the bottle of chilled Almadén on the pressboard coffee table between us and stared at each other. It was my move, but I had to make sure of one thing before I opened up to her.

"Joanne is the most angelic child I've ever seen," I said. "And you're a lucky mother, the way you can be with her full-time and still have your career."

"My *brilliant* career," she corrected me ruefully.

"It must be rough having to raise a child by yourself," I ventured. "Er—would I be out of line if I ask whether you're widowed or divorced?"

"Neither," she said. The playfulness was gone from her tone. She made the word sound like a door slamming in my face and seemed to be bracing herself for an unpleasant scene.

"Hold it a minute. I don't know why you think I asked you that question, but whatever you're thinking is wrong. Have I made a single offensive remark or even the slightest pass at you in all the times I've come here?"

"No," she conceded dubiously. "But that doesn't mean—"

"If I were bothered by an unmarried woman raising a child, would I have commissioned you to do these paintings?"

"Maybe you thought you were buying more than paintings. A lot of men have this sick idea that a woman with a child and without a husband has to be a hooker."

"Look at me," I told her. "Come on, right in the eyes like Joanne would. Now, do you honestly think I put out all this money as a buildup to propositioning you?"

"I . . . I guess not. I can't believe you'd be that stupid. You could rent a lot of flesh for what you've given me."

"Actually, I think I am going to make you an offer, but you have my word it's got nothing to do with sex. But first I have to know if there's a man who has any say in what you and Joanne do or where you go."

"Mr. Blake," she said, "my daughter and I have no one but each other, and much as I appreciate your business and much as I think I like you, we don't want a man in our lives."

"You and me against the world," I murmured.

"Hmmm?"

"The Helen Reddy number. You and Joanne remind me of that song." It was at that instant I made the decision. "Now," I said, "would you like to know why I've had you do those paintings?"

"I never thought you intended to hang them on your wall. That room and that woman obviously mean something special to you." She leaned closer on the love seat and reached for me with her eyes. "Whatever you tell me I promise to keep confidential."

I turned away from her, wondered if I were about to make the blunder of my life. *No,* the voice told me. *This woman is the right one.*

"My name isn't Blake," I began slowly. "It's Lattman. I'm a private investigator." I unpocketed my wallet and displayed my state license—or rather, a Lafferty rendition of such a document—handed her one of my professional cards. "The woman in the paintings was murdered back in May. The killer got away with making it look like an accident. My job is to nail him. I need you and Joanne to help."

The words poured out of me then for an hour or more, as if a dam inside me had crumbled to powder. The history of the Haskell family, the death of the patriarch and his long-lost daughter forty-eight hours apart, the hundred-twenty-hour clock—everything but two items. I didn't tell her that the woman who had died as Ann Haskell was an impostor and I didn't tell her who I was. I did give her a rough outline of my plan to trap the killer and of the roles she and Joanne were to play in the game.

"The man . . . the man who hired me has a lot of money, but—well, he says he has nothing to live for anymore. He doesn't care what the job costs. If you come in with me you and Joanne will live in decent comfort for a couple of years even if you never sell another painting. I, er, talked to the client about you last night. He's willing to advance you fifteen thousand dollars, and there will be another fifteen when it's over. Not bad for maybe two months of your time. Well, are you interested?"

I could almost hear the wheels whirring as with lips clamped tight and eyes squinched half shut she weighed the risks against the benefits. I counted the hours while she wrestled with herself. Did she dare trust me? Throw in her lot and her daughter's with a man who'd hired her under false pretenses? Join in the hunt for someone who had already murdered one woman horribly?

When she spoke again she seemed to have made up her mind, but I couldn't tell which way. "How much of this story can you prove to me?" she demanded.

"I can show you the newspaper reports of Ann Haskell's death. I have friends in the department, so I think I could get you a copy of the police file on the accident."

"Could I talk to your client before I commit myself?"

"No," I said too quickly. "The client—well, he told me he wouldn't talk to anyone but me about it. He's . . . well, a married man—a wealthy married man—he was having an affair with Miss Haskell and wanted to divorce his wife and—"

"Please don't lie to me, Mr. Lattman," she said. "You are not just a hired gun in this story. You knew that apartment and that woman too well. Those weren't a client's tears in your eyes when I was painting her."

I saw no point in extending that impromptu farce. "All right," I confessed. "Ann Haskell and I . . . I will never know another woman like her. There is no client. Just me."

"Thanks for your honesty." She slid over on the love seat toward me and extended her hand, which was damp with tension. "I'll work with you, Mr. Lattman. But only as long as I am absolutely certain that my child is not in the slightest danger. If I even think Joanne may be hurt, we drop out that minute. And we keep your advance too."

"That's fair," I said. "There won't be any danger. We're going to be protected by a security guard agency all the way. And you needn't worry about sexual advances from me. This game is complicated enough already."

"This game is complicated," she said, "like Picasso was talented."

New York continued to groan through an enervating summer, but most of the preparations for our own Normandy invasion were carried out in air-conditioned comfort. I rented a suite for Suzy and Joanne in an apartment hotel a block from me on Central Park South and strolled over every morning to rehearse them in and accustom them to their new roles as the second wife and the daughter of Mr. Edward P. Blake. They grew into their parts beautifully. Before long Suzy was helping me concoct her own biography and mine. Joanne's ecstasy at the fabulous game we were playing was unbounded, and she took to me as her daddy with the wild delight of a child who in real life had never known a father. Soon she was running into my outstretched arms and giving me a big moist hug every time I poked my head through the door of their suite. I almost wished that she and Suzy

131

really were my family. Keep feeling that way, I told myself. Makes you more natural in the part.

Most afternoons and evenings I devoted to working with Lafferty in his well-cooled pad on Minetta Street. We toiled with the care of medieval Japanese artisans over the documents that created three lives out of nothing. Paper history for Edward Peter Blake. Marriage certificate dated 1977 between that gentleman and one Ann Haskell, with the lady's signature courtesy of the lease she had signed on the apartment where she'd died. (Having that paper photocopied on the sneak had cost me a piddling ten-spot.) Birth certificate, dated thirteen and a half months later, for Joanne Denise Blake, daughter of Edward Peter and Ann Haskell Blake. Divorce decree and property settlement between Edward Peter Blake and Ann Haskell Blake, dated approximately half a year after the child's birth, with custody of the kid awarded by consent of both parties to the father. Another marriage certificate, bearing a date just short of a year after the divorce, attesting to the union in lawful wedlock of Edward Peter Blake and Suzanne French. Adoption papers granting Suzanne French Blake legal status as the substitute mother of Joanne Denise Blake. Each of these masterpieces of the forger's art went in due course and with the payment of appropriate bribes into the niche in the public records which it would have occupied had the event attested actually taken place. Piece by piece the groundwork for the invasion was laid. By the end of July I was ready for a sortie into the target area.

That Tuesday morning I caught a cab to LaGuardia and grabbed a seat in coach on TWA's early nonstop to Saint Louis. I had phoned ahead for two appointments, one as Edward P. Blake and the other as the unadorned and quintessential me. An airport cab shot me from Lambert International to the Slavin Building, a low-rise office block on Bonhomme in the heart of the Clayton business district. David Keel, Esq. maintained a roost on the third floor, a quiet shop with nondescript functional chairs and carpeting and office furniture. Lawbooks bulged on Bro Dart shelving along the broad inner corridor and on all four walls of his sanctum. Keel was a runt in his mid thirties, his dome warmed by a rug that kept shimmying in the current from the room's air conditioning duct. We discussed in detail the case on which I'd retained him, I turned over the documentation he'd asked me to bring and the first check for his services, and he promised that within a week at most he would file a petition under Section 472.150 of the Missouri Probate Code, requesting the probate division of the circuit court to vacate its prior order admitting the will of Bradford W. Haskell to probate and to enter a new order awarding one third of the decedent's residuary estate to Joanne Denise Blake, a minor, through her guardians Edward Peter Blake and Suzanne French Blake.

That wound up half my Saint Louis business for the day. I left Keel's office and found a phone in the downstairs lobby and called a cab company. A red and black clunker picked me up in front of the Slavin Building ten minutes later and jounced east on the Forest Park Expressway and then on Market to downtown Saint Louis. I paid the jockey in front of a tall building at Eighth and Olive and stepped into a cool dim terrazzo-floored corridor lined with clothing and antique stores. The elevator at the rear of the corridor might have been new around the time of the Saint Louis World's Fair, in 1904. The wheezing monster coughed me out on seven. Most of the office doors I passed in the upper hallway seemed to belong to lawyers or accountants. I twisted the knob of the oddball labeled EAGLE EYE INVESTIGATIONS • ENTER and found myself in a reception room bone-bare of human beings. My watch read 11:42. Someone was enjoying an early lunch.

I heard sounds of altercation blasting from behind a closed door at the rear of the suite and followed the racket to a fumed-oak slab marked FILE ROOM and knocked. The voices kept yammering undiminished, then snapped off abruptly as a light going out. I walked in.

There wasn't a file cabinet in sight. The room was lined with steel shelving and the shelves were lined with videocassettes. In the semidarkness I could see a six-foot-square projection TV screen against one wall, with the chunky wood-grain cube that made up the sending unit in the middle of the room and a video recorder squatting on its top surface. A trim fiftyish fellow with gray hair hanging over his eyebrows in 1960s mod fashion sprang out of a canvas director's chair and whipped on the overheads and bounced over to pump my hand. He looked like an elf in a denim leisure suit.

"Ah!" he beamed. "The legendary Mr. Turner! What a pleasure to meet a man of your eminence in the profession!"

"And you must be the fabulous Mr. Zwack," I responded with the same hyperdramatic intonation, "the Sam Spade of Saint Louis, renowned in song and story. May I ask what all that racket was?"

"We-e-ell, this is one of those quiet days at the office," he explained, "and when things are dull I tend to fill in time watching the exploits of my mythical brethren on videocassette."

"You mean you groove on . . . ?"

"Private eye movies!" He spoke the words as if only fools didn't share his avocation. "I have all the Philip Marlowes, every one of the three versions of *The Maltese Falcon, Kiss Me Deadly* with Ralph Meeker as Mike Hammer. I honestly believe I have the finest collection of its kind in the world. I was just running a little dandy called *Too Many Winners*.

"Never heard of it," I said.

"Released by PRC Pictures in nineteen forty-seven, starring Hugh Beaumont as Mike Shayne. Beaumont of course went on to fame and fortune in the fifties as the father in the *Leave It To Beaver* TV series. He died just a few months ago and I've been screening his private eye movies again as a sort of memorial."

"Picture any good?"

"We-e-ell, it was directed by William Beaudine," he said, "and Beaudine's work is rarely better than competent. But on the other hand, it's rarely worse either." He tucked his arm in mine and gentled me out of the file room. "As long as you're early, let's go to lunch."

We went down and joined the chaotic downtown pedestrian traffic for the walk of a few blocks to a coffee shop on Tucker Boulevard. Zwack ordered the chef salad. When it came, with a gravy boat of Russian dressing on the side, he poured the thick reddish goo over his lettuce and cheese and ham and turkey and tomato wedges and then pulled a clear plastic pill cylinder out of his leisure suit's breast pocket and sprinkled a brownish stuff like fine sawdust all over his lunch. "Bran," he said. "I put it on everything I eat. Keeps me regular. It's especially good on bacon cheeseburgers, if you'd like to try some on yours?"

"Thanks," I said, trying not to shudder visibly, "but you'll need the rest for your coffee."

Over his rabbit food Zwack lobbed a crazy angel grin at me. "So dear old Jock recommended Eagle Eye to be your security agency while you're in town! It's been *ages* since that wonderful brogue warmed my ears. Now, tell me why you need a bodyguard, and I just hope it's the kind of wild tale clients always tell the private eyes in movies."

In movies, and in PI novels too for that matter, the client always starts out by lying to the shamus through his or more frequently through her teeth. So far I had lied through mine to every person involved in the operation, including my newly hatched wife and child, but the one individual I'd made up my mind not to ensnare with a whopper was Zwack. First of all because he was a veteran of the confidence profession and came recommended without qualification by the Jock, and secondly because I knew the man couldn't do the job I expected of him unless he was in on the script. As I spun the story his eyes became more and more excited, the intervals between forkfuls of bran-seasoned salad ever longer. This strange little bird who worshipped the mythology of his latest career was finding himself smack in the middle of an intrigue more bizarre than anything in his videocassette collection, and God, how he loved it! We took a very long lunch that day. When he finished his salad we still had much to talk over, so he ordered a plate of strawberry ice cream for dessert and, sure enough, polluted that cool pink mound with the rest of his pill bottle of bran. We debated which hotel would be the best for my "family" and me to patronize during our excursion to Saint Louis and settled on the Centurion Inn, a modernistic high rise just off Interstate 70 near the airport. We worked out the details of the security plan. We negotiated over how much this brainstorm of mine was going to cost me beyond the expenses, which were sure to be astronomical all by themselves. And as we dawdled over third cups of coffee I broached the possibility of another assignment, which had come into my head during this morning's westbound flight.

"How much do you know," I asked him, "about the other PIs in the Saint Louis area?"

"We-e-ell, we shamuses don't hobnob as much as

doctors and lawyers do, but I have a shrewd idea who my competitors are. Why do you ask?"

"I want you to find one of your colleagues for me," I said. "I'm not sure he comes from here and I'm not even sure he exists. But remember how Jeffrey Haskell threatened to have a private snoop investigate his so-called half sister?"

"Of course. And you want to find out if he followed through?"

"More than that. The last time she and I were together, she told me she thought she'd been shadowed for the past few days. She described the guy as tall and skinny, with a high widow's peak in the shape of the letter M. Does that sound like any Saint Louis investigator you know?"

He chewed on the description as he poked at his gums with a toothpick. "No one around here looks like that," he said. "Of course, since the lady came from New York and was going back to New York after her visit here, it would be more sensible if he'd hired a New York detective for the job. That is, if he hired anyone at all."

"Any way you can find out if he hired someone?"

"It's possible," he said with judicious nonchalance, "although I can't promise results overnight. I take it you'd like to interview this fellow if I can find him?"

"It depends. If he was hired just to check her background and shadow her, I want to know whether he was watching her place that Friday night and Saturday morning when she . . . when she . . ."

"I understand." He put down the coffee spoon he'd been tapping against his empty cup during my dialogue and pointed the forefinger of his delicate hand at me like a third grade teacher correcting a backward pupil. "But I have this strange notion that you've contradicted yourself. First you said that the man who paid to have your lady wasted was Jeff Haskell. Now you tell me that he may also have paid a detective who might well have had the lady's apartment under surveillance precisely when the hit man made his call! Surely if this Haskell had an ounce of sense he wouldn't have had the killer go in while the place was watched by another of his emissaries."

"This kill had to be done in a hurry," I reminded him. "A minute after the hundred-twenty-hour clock stopped running and it would be too late. He may have screwed up the coordination. But remember, I said that I wanted to find out if this detective was watching the place Friday night and Saturday morning *only if* he was hired just to check her out and trail her around. There's another possibility."

"Which is?"

"That the private eye he sent to follow her was also the hit man he sent to kill her," I said.

TWELVE

Literary warriors write of the joy of going into combat, the thrill of risk, the delirious keenness with which one lives when one knows that each minute may be the last. There are people both in and out of uniform who choose that sort of existence. I am not one of them. I am a bookish introvert, scared shitless in those rare moments of danger I encounter. I sit on the sidelines and spin my webs. I shun battle zones like the black plague.

I am also a shameless liar.

From the notebooks of Milo Turner

Another week of touch up work back in New York and I was ready to launch my own version of D Day. The excitement started to get to me. I had to sip three or four ounces of Dewar's to put me out each night. Everything depended on the timing of events in Saint Louis, which I couldn't control and didn't dare to seem anxious about. I cut back on my daily visits to Suzy and Joanne and spent my time staring at idiocy on the tube and begging the phone in my condo to ring.

And finally it did.

"Yes, everything's in order, Mr. Blake. The petition was filed in the Probate Division yesterday and I sent a copy to your address." Not the George Boyd condo of course, but an accommodation address I'd given Keel, complete with a phone number, which was connected to the Central Park South phone by a call-forwarding device.

"And you served copies on the Haskell brothers?"

"Naturally. On Jeffrey, in his capacity as executor of the estate, and on both Jeffrey and Eugene, in their capacities as residuary legatees."

"I suppose it's too soon to expect any reaction from them yet."

"It won't take them long to get in touch, with this much property at stake," he predicted. "I'll let you know as soon as they do."

"Fine. And remember what I told you to say. My wife and daughter and I plan to be in Saint Louis soon on a combination business trip and vacation and I'll be happy to discuss the case with them at that time."

"I'll tell them of your desire for a conference, of course," Keel said. "But I've already made it clear to you, Mr. Blake, that in my professional opinion it's *extremely* premature to have a settlement discussion even before the court sets a hearing date."

"It has to be done this way," I insisted. "I'll explain my reasons in full when I see you in Saint Louis." Such was my polite rendition of the underlying message to him: *Do it my way or some other lawyer will.* I had specified an attorney who was unaccustomed to multimillion-dollar litigation precisely because I had to have some leverage over him, and there is no better leverage than the fear of being kicked off the biggest case in one's career.

"If you insist . . . " He sighed with the resignation of a Buddhist monk, and broke the connection.

Three days later he was on the horn again to report that he had heard the lion roar. Jeffrey Haskell had called, and the dialogue between the two barristers had been, as Keel put it, difficult. "But I explained our position thoroughly," he said, "and invited him over to examine your documentation."

"Did he take you up on it?"

"I spent most of this morning with him."

"And told him I wanted a conference as soon as possible?"

"More subtly than that," Keel said, "but he got the message."

"What did he say?"

"He didn't rule it out."

"Call him back," I instructed. "Tell him my family and I will be in Saint Louis next week. Set up a definite appointment."

He called me again less than an hour later and told me that we had a date. Tuesday of next week, ten thirty in the morning in the offices of the legal department of Haskell's Supermarkets.

The minute Keel hung up I was on the phone to TWA, making three reservations, two adults and one child, in the nonsmoking section of the late afternoon nonstop to Saint Louis that would depart in less than forty-eight hours. With seats confirmed I dialed Eagle Eye Investigations and told Zwack when we'd arrive, then called Suzy at the apartment hotel a block away and gave her the word to start packing.

And so as the sun began its slide down the western sky that muggy Friday, the wide-body jet from LaGuardia touched tarmac at Lambert International Airport and dropped myself and my newly minted wife and daughter and a planeful of other passengers in the kill zone. I kept the three of us in the middle of a knot of deplaning travelers, not that we were at risk this early in the operation when the enemy didn't know we'd arrived, but just on general principles.

As we stepped out of the movable Jetway corridor into

the terminal proper I glanced around the area for a friendly face. And found one without even trying. Lounging nonchalantly in a scoop-bottomed plastic seat not a dozen feet from where we stood was Luther Zwack himself, an evening paper folded in his lap, a flight bag on the orange carpet next to his neatly polished cowboy boots. Without the smallest sign that he'd seen us he rose gracefully and hefted his bag and slipped into the crowd of newcomers to the Gateway to the West just a few people behind us. Suzy and Joanne and I followed the arrows through a maze of turnings to the cold metallic baggage claim area and waited in front of the ovoid carousel for our suitcases to be spewed up. That dear gnome had promised security from the moment we touched down and was living up to his word. We eyed the motley assortment of luggage leaping off the escalator ramp onto the carousel's steel plates and I wondered how many of the people lined up along the edge of the clanking monster worked for Zwack. The boss man himself was nowhere to be seen.

The preordered rental Cutlass was waiting for us at the Avis counter on the airport's lower level. With our gear crammed in the back and ourselves in the front seat we took the five-minute hop to the steel and glass slab known as the Centurion Inn. The desk had our reservations in order. Mr. and Mrs. Edward P. Blake and child were assigned to suite 810, a living room-bedroom unit just a few steps from the enclosed concrete fire stairs. I had insisted on that location when I'd phoned ahead for the rooms. "My wife's been terrified ever since those hotel fires in Las Vegas," I'd explained, and the reservations clerk had understood perfectly and was happy to oblige.

There was at least an hour's worth of daylight and Joanne was too keyed up by her first airplane flight to even think about going to bed yet. "You promised to give me swimming lessons if the hotel had a pool, Mother, and I saw the sign in the lobby and it *does*!" So having already dined at 32,000 feet, we freshened up and changed into swimwear and rode the bubble elevator to the third-floor pool deck. Suzy had treated herself and Joanne to matching blue maillots and scarlet beach robes for the trip. They stripped off the robes and leapt squealing into the bright water, and I kept in character only by means of a stern reminder to myself that a married man does not sneak lascivious looks at his wife's bathing-suited bod. But God, she was lovely.

I paddled around with Joanne in the shallow end of the pool while Suzy climbed out and scampered to the diving board and lifted her arms and made a graceful arc and a wild splash and swam underwater back to us and bobbed up and tossed her head back and threw her arms around her child and took her hands and towed her to the center of the pool. I stood to the side beaming like papa, proud as Joanne clung to her mother's hands and kicked her feet out behind her with cries of joy. Memory stabbed me: a pool in the yard of an Arizona ranch house, a golden-tan child swimming like a fish in the sparkling blue water, twenty-three summers ago. I pushed the image back into the darkness, made myself look around casually at the other people who were enjoying a twilight dip.

There weren't more than eight or nine in the water besides my family and me, and all of them had been there before us. The only ones who had come down to the pool behind us were a dumpy-looking man and woman in their forties who were reclining in lounge chairs on the concrete deck. Long-married couple, their appearance seemed to say. Comfortable with each other as a pair of old shoes. When the man noticed that I was glancing in his direction he dipped into his bathing trunks pocket and dug out a crumpled green pack of mentholated cigarettes. He stuck one in his wife's mouth and another in his own and pulled a disposable plastic lighter out of her beach bag on the top of the poolside table next to their loungers and ignited first his coffin nail and then hers. That was the sequence of signals. The dumpies were from Eagle Eye Investigations.

I climbed up the ladder out of the pool and sauntered casually past them just as the man pulled a room key out of his trunks pocket and laid it atop the cigarette pack. Seven oh nine, the tag read. Zwack had done it again. Their room was one floor below ours and almost as close to the fire stairs as 810. We had agreed after studying the hotel's floor plan that the people who were going to protect us inside and around the Centurion Inn should be based no more than three levels from us and that we should all be a few steps from the concrete staircase for quick movement between rooms.

Thus began our precombat breather. A guidebook plus recollections of a few earlier professional visits to the Saint Louis area helped me map our itinerary. Saturday we sweltered with ten thousand other tourists, strolling along cobblestoned Wharf Street with the muddy Mississippi a pebble's toss away, boarding the lopsided Ferris wheel car that lifted us six hundred feet to the observation platform atop the Gateway Arch, taking a waterborne tour of the riverfront on the *Samuel Clemens*. Sunday we visited the Missouri Botanical Gardens and the dinosaur statues in the grounds of the Museum of Science and crowned the day with a few hours at the Magic House. Monday, when almost every rival attraction is closed, we merged into another DeMille–size mob at the Forest Park zoo and watched our child—every minute with her made me feel that much more paternal—as she waved at the orangutans in the ape house and blew kisses at the lions of Big Cat Country and caressed the baby animals in the petting center.

Our sleeping arrangements at the hotel would have pleased a monk. Suzy and Joanne shared the bedroom, I camped on the living room couch. They slept well. I dozed fitfully, listening to the seconds tick away toward ten thirty Tuesday morning when I would have my first face-to-face meeting with the man who had killed my woman.

D Day dawned gray and sullen with rain clouds blotting out the sky. As prearranged, David Keel buzzed the suite from downstairs a few minutes after nine, and I left Suzy and Joanne to breakfast on room service and joined our legal beagle in the Centurion coffee shop for sausage, scrambled, and a strategy session. The ladies met us in the lobby at ten, I introduced Keel to the wife and daughter, and the four of us piled into his Buick station wagon with personalized license plates reading LAWYR. He took us south along Hanley into the heart of the Clayton business district, keeping up a stream of small talk with Suzy about techniques of rearing children, a species of which he himself had three. We squeezed into a visitor slot in the parking lot behind a gleaming seven-story office building on Bemiston and got inside the front door moments before the first thunderclap.

I glanced at the lobby directory as we waited for an elevator. The building was the headquarters of Haskell's Supermarkets, Inc., and the legal department seemed to have the sixth floor to itself. The sleek cage whooshed us up and deposited us in a reception area carpeted in green velour and presided over by a stunning redhead behind a fortress desk. She and Joanne exchanged innocent smiles and a cool handshake. Then the receptionist escorted us into a walnut-paneled conference room with recessed lighting and silk window drapes and a long table buffed to high gloss. Six cushioned chairs were arranged along each side of the table and each position was equipped with a yellow legal pad, a Datamate pen, and a crystal goblet filled with ice water and a thin slice of lime. We sat in the four middle chairs on one side and gave each other reassuring glances and waited for something to happen. The only action was the thunderstorm outside. "Good psychology," Keel whispered to me. "Keep us waiting, put us on edge." He took out a pocket mirror and adjusted his toupee and then began cracking his knuckles against the table edge.

In the middle of that routine the door opened and in they trooped. A trio, two men and a woman, who entered last and shut the door gently behind them. They marched in like three West Point plebes drilling on the parade ground and stood in front of their chairs. Keel and I rose from ours, Suzy and Joanne stayed sitting. Keel did the introductions. Nobody bothered to shake hands.

"I'm Jeff Haskell." The head of the corporate legal department had a Gestapo interrogator's face, a Lech Walesa mustache, a voice like a bucket of rusty nails. So this was the bastard who had paid a hit man to waste my lady. For a few seconds I screamed silently to heaven for a .357 Magnum to materialize in my hand so I could pump half a dozen holes into that six-hundred-dollar vested suit.

"Gene Haskell. I'm with the Saint Louis Symphony Orchestra." Jeff's little brother was thin as a consumptive, with soft and sensitive features, eyes that darted nervously behind gold-rimmed specs, hands aflutter. I was amazed that such a walking palpitation could handle the concert violin. So this was the wimp whose life had been saved when my lady walked into the picture and shifted Jeffrey's target from his brother to herself. It wouldn't have needed a hit man to arrange an accident to little Gene. Jeff could take a deep breath and blow him into the path of an oncoming car.

"I'm Daria Shore. Deputy director of the legal department." She was a tall intense woman of about thirty with high cheekbones and gaunt face and starved-looking fashion model body. Her hair was ink black and styled boyishly like the young Audrey Hepburn's. I remembered something from that last love night before my lady died, something she'd said about Gene Haskell. "He's engaged to a young woman lawyer, one of those wire and whipcord bitches." This could be the one. I sneaked a glance at her ring finger and saw it ablaze with diamond sparks.

"Let's get to business," Jeffrey croaked, and in unison the enemy trio sat. "Keel, this meeting was your idea, and we're all busy people here, so why don't you make your pitch?"

Which was Suzy's cue to lean forward and smile winningly at the Genghis Khan of the legal staff. "Mr. Haskell, we did want you to meet us personally, but is there someplace I could wait with Joanne while you all talk? I don't think she'd be terribly interested in the discussion."

"Peggy loves children," Daria Shore suggested in a voice like the music of Oriental temple chimes. "She's the receptionist you saw as you got out of the elevator. Why not leave the child with her? You'll want to take part in the meeting yourself, of course." I read that last remark as the exhortation of a professional woman to a female of uncertain credentials not to let the cause of liberation down. Suzy and Joanne excused themselves and stepped out hand in hand, and a minute later Suzy was back and in her chair. I nodded at David Keel to begin.

My gunfighter snapped open his attaché case, made three piles of various legal papers, and shoved one across the walnut to each of the opposition. Then he began talking, and a masterful spiel it was. His knowledge of the facts I had concocted was encyclopedic, his research of judicial precedent exhaustive, his oratorical style on a par with what I'd had in mind when I asked the Jock to find me a tiger at the bargaining table. He spoke of the life and work of his client Edward P. Blake, whose business was the purchase, rehabilitation, and resale of residential housing. He told of the marriage in 1977 between Mr. Blake and the late Ann Haskell. In euphemistic language he conceded that the match had not been a howling success. Ann was restless, haunted by dreams of independence and a career of her own, more unhappy in her marriage with each passing day.

"A lot of women felt that way in the seventies," Keel said, as if for the benefit of any of us who hadn't been alive in those bygone times. "The aspirations of the feminist movement tore a whole generation of women apart. Mrs. Blake began"—he darted a glance at me, perhaps asking me to forgive his bluntness—"she began drinking too much, to dull the pain. There were a few— well, periods of separation."

"Always her idea," I cut in poignantly. "I never stopped wanting and loving her. She always came back after a few weeks, and I always took her back."

"Then," Keel went on, "very unexpectedly, Mrs. Blake became pregnant. Joanne was born in nineteen seventy-eight. One might have thought having responsibility for a child would have—helped her resolve this terrible conflict. Well, it didn't. Six months after Joanne was born she . . . Mr. Blake, how do I say this without hurting you?"

"Try the plain and simple way." I did my best not to be hammy as I went into my fight-back-the-tears routine. "Six months after our daughter was born Ann walked out on her and me and the marriage. For keeps. She left me to raise an infant without any help. Well, I lucked out." I reached blindly for Suzy's hand and she gave mine a reassuring squeeze. "I met the present Mrs. Blake and married her. No one could have done a finer job of raising a child who wasn't her own flesh and blood. Joanne accepts Suzy as her real mother and has no memory of . . . of my first wife at all." I threw in that last tidbit on impulse, just in case the kid said the wrong thing to the redheaded receptionist outside.

Jeff Haskell clapped his hands sardonically. "A damn good story," he said like a bullterrier with a sore throat. "Maybe you can sell it to one of the networks and they can adapt it into an evening soap."

"I fail to understand that crack." Keel smiled faintly and touched his skull rug like a lucky charm. "You've seen copies of the marriage certificate, Joanne's birth certificate, the divorce decree giving Mr. Blake custody of the child, the second marriage certificate, and the adoption decree. Surely you don't doubt their authenticity?" After the fortune I had paid to have those documents forged and filed, I said to myself, they had damn well better not doubt them.

"That isn't our problem," Daria Shore replied for the team in the manner of a take-charge lady who could run Haskell's Supermarkets, Inc. single-handed if she had to. "I believe what Mr. Haskell means is that when—I'm not sure what to call her—when Ann came out to Ladue to visit her father a couple of weeks before—well, before both of them passed away, she never once mentioned having been married or having had a child. Did she, Gene?"

"Not once, dear," the fiddler whispered in a scared-rabbit voice. Which seemed to confirm my hunch that they were engaged. But I couldn't help wondering what the lawyer lady with the fine-boned face might conceivably see in that repressed little nerd. Surely a woman with her dynamism and potential wouldn't betray the cause by marrying a man for his money! "I assumed that she was single, childless, and unattached. Didn't you, Jeff?"

"She never said so point blank," the older brother rasped, "but that was my impression. And I'll tell you another thing. If she had a drinking problem she kept that well concealed, too, while she was here. I don't recall her taking more than a glass of wine and maybe a little brandy or liqueur."

At which juncture David Keel countered with a verbal punch of his own. "Well, it's natural enough that she wouldn't have volunteered the information about her, ah, family situation. After all, gentlemen, your own father's first wife, Ann Haskell's mother, walked out on *her* husband back in the late nineteen forties. If Ann had revealed that she too had deserted her man, she might have alienated your father irrevocably, and she came to Saint Louis of course to—well, to make up with him while there was still time."

"Oh, bullshit," Jeff roared. "She came here to find out if she was in his will."

Keel responded with a good-natured shrug. "Well, she's not my client, and she's not here to tell us her motives, which are irrelevant anyway. Your father executed a perfectly valid and unassailable will leaving his daughter Ann one third of his residuary. If Ann had lived just a few more days, we wouldn't be having this dispute now. She would have been absolutely entitled to her legacy."

"But she got drunk and cracked her skull open," Jeff broke in brutally, "forty-eight hours after Pop died. Probably she was celebrating her good fortune." With my hand still entwined in Suzy's I could feel her shudder at the son-of-a-bitch's callousness.

"How the accident happened is also irrelevant," Keel said calmly. "She died within one hundred twenty hours of your father. Now ordinarily, of course, that would have nullified the bequest to her, and you and your brother would split the residuary, fifty fifty. But, as you've now seen in the flesh, Ann Haskell was survived by a child, who has outlived Bradford Haskell already by a lot longer than the one hundred twenty hours the law requires. Joanne falls within the antilapse exception to the general rule. She is entitled to the one-third share that her mother would have taken had she survived Bradford Haskell by one hundred twenty hours."

"That's what you say," Jeffrey snarled.

Throughout the lawyerly dialogue I had sat back and watched the faces of the terrible trio as intensely as possible without being obvious about it. The one I studied closest of all was Jeff's. I was waiting for something to show in his cold gray eyes, waiting for his mouth to go slack, for a sheen of guilt sweat. I wanted to see some sign of what I hoped and prayed had been roaring through his head ever since he'd been served with Keel's legal papers: *Oh my God. I killed her for nothing.* What I saw was fury and frustration and all the other emotions natural in a man who was watching one and two-thirds million dollars slipping through his fingers like a greased pig. Stare hard as I might, I could see no looks that clearly signaled guilt. The man had iron control.

"But we're going to contest you," big brother went on, swiping at the soup strainer under his nose.

"Your privilege," Keel said coolly, "but you can't possibly have grounds." He spoke with the faith of a preacher of the one true religion, fulfilling superbly the other criterion I had set out to the Jock: that my lawyer had to be a pussycat when it came to believing my whoppers.

"Try fraud," Jeff shot back at him. "You practically admitted it yourself, Keel. If Ann had told Pop that she'd deserted her family, Pop would probably have disinherited her. As far as I'm concerned, her concealing those facts constitutes fraud, and the kid's claim is tainted the same way her own would be if she were alive."

That was an argument we hadn't foreseen, and it triggered another donnybrook among the lawyers. But Keel was equal to the occasion. With a controlled fury that he could obviously turn on and off like a faucet, he insisted that not volunteering a potentially damaging biographical fact wasn't legally on all fours with actively misrepresenting a matter that might lead to disinheritance. I stayed out of the fight. I sipped lime-flavored ice water from my goblet, watched the thunderstorm between the silk drapes, shot glances at Daria Shore, sitting erect and queenly and above the battle, and at Gene Haskell, shuffling the papers on the walnut in front of him like a man dreadfully embarrassed by the nonsense. Lawyers thrive on that kind of scrap. It is by first generating such bouts and then slugging them out that the profession makes its profit. I let the combatants go on for about ten minutes, then when the duel gave no sign of dying away I made my move.

"Gentlemen, gentlemen, *please*!" I all but shouted. "I'm sorry we've gotten into a fight. Look, the reason I suggested this conference is that I'd like to avoid long-drawn-out litigation if possible. The only thing I'm interested in is my daughter's future. She . . . she doesn't even remember her biological mother and I don't want to expose her to a lot of dirt about Ann." I tried simultaneously to shed and fight back tears of remembrance. "She didn't treat us right but . . . " I felt a wad of tissue in the hand that was still joined to Suzy's and used it to wipe and I hoped redden my eyes. "But a part of me still loves her very much. I'm willing—that is, Suzy and I as Joanne's legal guardians are willing to settle for substantially less than a third of the residuary estate. I make

152

good money in the housing business, Suzy's a fine artist. We don't need all that much to take care of Joanne."

"So what will you settle for?" Daria Shore asked, stepping down from her throne to where the action was.

"Twenty per cent?" I suggested.

"That's two million goddamn dollars!" big brother bellowed.

"The child is entitled," Keel reminded the adversary gently, "to three and a third million, more or less. If you settle, you each receive roughly six hundred sixty-six thousand dollars extra, and we avoid a costly lawsuit too. Are you interested in pursuing this subject?"

"I am," Gene Haskell mumbled. He gave the impression that he'd do anything in the world including mutilate himself if only he could be released from this dissonant mess and get back to practicing the Khachaturian G Major Violin Concerto. But Jeff's simultaneous boom came close to drowning out the younger brother's Milquetoast response.

"We can discuss that later," he said. "I'm going to need a few weeks to have private detectives investigate this whole story."

"Private detectives?" Keel echoed uncertainly. "What in the world do you want private detectives for?"

Jeffrey flashed a frosty smile at him, with the mouth alone. "I won't make any statement at this time that would be slanderous if I should be wrong," he said, "but there just may be more fraud here than I realized at first." He scraped back his chair and lurched to his feet with little brother and future sister-in-law doing likewise a split second behind him. Outside, thunder blasted again, but the bells of joy in my head were sounding even louder. The threat of private peepers. That was exactly how he'd reacted when the supposed Ann Haskell had entered the picture. God, God, now if only I can keep him on course!

The meeting broke up minus smiles and handshakes. While Keel stuffed his briefcase with legal papers under the triple stare of the players on the other side, I announced nonchalantly that my family and I were staying at the Centurion Inn, in case anyone needed to get in touch with us. That information planted, Keel and Suzy and I exited the conference room and marched back to the reception area. Joanne was perched on the edge of the redhead's desk and chattering away about all the different kinds of simians she'd seen yesterday at the zoo. "Spiders and squirrels and guenons and vervets and hamadryas baboons and orangutans . . . " We thanked the flame-haired lady for serving as an impromptu day care center and basked in her assurance that Joanne was a darling, fascinating to listen to. The elevator dropped us to ground level and we marched out of the human zoo into the sweet and friendly storm.

Which, by the time Keel braked his station wagon in the loading area by the entrance to the Centurion, had fallen off to a dribble, with faint growls of thunder fading away to the east. As the ladies were getting out of the back seat and I was fumbling with the handle of the front passenger door, the lawyer tugged urgently at my left wrist. "I have to talk with you alone," he whispered.

Having not the faintest notion what was bothering the man, I nodded unobtrusively and asked Suzy to take Joanne upstairs and find something on TV for her to watch. "I'll be up right away," I promised. When they were inside the building Keel U-turned and swung into the guest parking lot, found a vacant slot wide enough to accommodate his wheels, and shut the engine off.

"Now," he said, "perhaps you'll explain to me, Mr. Blake, why you were so eager to compromise an unassailable claim even before a hearing date has been set."

His face and tone told me that he wasn't asking out of abstract curiosity. The man was seething with suppressed anger. The Milonic brain raced. I couldn't give him my real reason and I couldn't let Keel slip his leash. What would he buy that was consistent with every other lie I'd sold him? Then I saw it.

"All right." I sighed stoically. "I guess you're entitled to know. Thanks for not asking me in front of Joanne."

"What does the child have to do with it?"

"Did . . . did you notice that Joanne and I don't look terribly much alike?" I asked him.

"Well, yes, but so what? My own sons don't bear the least resemblance to me, but they've got their mother's eyes and mouth. I assume your child looks like her mother too."

"I'm—I'm not saying this right, it's not easy to talk about. . . . Look, you remember I told you about the—the temporary vacations Ann took from our marriage?"

"Of course."

"Well, I think it's . . . it's possible that during those times she was . . . " I hesitated for what I hoped was just the right interval. "Sleeping with another man or men," I finished in a frantic rush to spit the sentence out of my mouth. "The last time she went away and came back to me and we got together again, well, it was about three weeks later that she missed her period. Joanne was born eight months or so afterward. I—I literally don't know if I'm the child's biological father or not!"

It was stifling in that station wagon with the windows up, and the windshield was foggy with our breath. Keel dug a rag out of the glove compartment and wiped the glass clean, giving me time to recover my composure, which I had to admit was damn decent of him. He stowed the rag away and twisted around behind the steering wheel to face me as best he could.

"Ann—uh, the first Mrs. Blake never told you whether she was, well, faithful while she was away?"

"She never told me anything about those times. I was trying to save the marriage, so I didn't push her."

"So," he said, massaging his chin furiously, his toupee shimmering with the head motion. "Okay, Mr. Blake, I appreciate your telling me. Legally it doesn't affect our claim in the least. When a married woman bears a child, it is presumed that the woman's husband is the child's father. That's the strongest presumption known to the law, so powerful that it's saddled a lot of men with the obligation to support kids their wives conceived with outside lovers."

"But suppose Haskell puts private detectives to work and they discover—well, let's say they find out what Ann's blood type was and they make Joanne and me give them blood samples and it turns out they're incompatible with my being Joanne's father?" In fact, that was one of the few unfixable weaknesses in my plan, and I was gambling that events would break too fast for the enemy to pursue the issue.

"Mr. Blake, I don't give a shit if it's biologically impossible for you to be the girl's father. The presumption stands. Our system will not tolerate casting doubt on the legitimacy of a child born to a married woman."

"Well," I said, "that's good to know, but even so I don't want Joanne exposed to hearing that kind of—dirt about her mother. I still want a quick settlement, even for a lot less money."

"Fine," he beamed. "So let's let this situation work for us instead of against us, okay?"

"What do you have in mind?"

"When I get back to my office," he said, "I'm going to phone Haskell and, er, clarify your settlement offer. It's good until twelve noon two weeks from today, then it's automatically withdrawn. Right after that phone conversation I'll dictate a letter to the same effect, which will go out to Haskell in the afternoon mail. In that length of time I don't think his detectives will have a chance in hell of digging up any skeletons."

Once again I wished myself hearty congratulations on my specifications for a lawyer. Not only would Keel's gambit reduce the risk to my scam but it would force the enemy to move quickly if they were going to act at all. Then on the spur of the instant I thought of an extra little fillip and went for it.

"When you talk to Haskell," I said, "tell him my family and I will be at the Centurion until two weeks from today and that the settlement offer is withdrawn unless they accept it before we go back to New York."

"That's even better," Keel said, a sentiment with which I couldn't have agreed more. I thanked him for the ride and his legal ingenuity and pumped his hand and slammed the station wagon door and trotted across puddle-dappled pavement to the side entrance to the inn.

Upstairs on the couch my family awaited me, giggling joyously as if they shared a secret from which the rest of the world was excluded. "Hi, Daddy," Suzy called across the living room as I turned the dead bolt behind me. "What did you think of our performances?"

"Tony caliber," I said. "Both of you. Special award to you, Joanne, for best kid in the business. Did you enjoy it?"

"I never realized before how creative it can be just to pretend you're someone else," Suzy said. "It's . . . well, it's like when I'm painting something and I can feel it coming alive under my brush."

"It was *fun!*" Joanne echoed, full of delight. "You play the best games I've ever played, Mr. Lattman. Couldn't you be my father all the time?"

Leave it to a precocious uninhibited kid to say the wrong thing at the wrong moment. "Well, at least for another two weeks, dear," I promised, and then turned helplessly to Suzy and added a remark which under the circumstances more than matched Joanne's for idiocy. "After that I guess it's up to your mother."

A flush crept up Suzy's face from her lovely tanned neck, and her eyes darted around the room as if she were looking for a way out of a trap. After what seemed like half an hour of awkward silence she found a mildly graceful escape route. "Was there a problem just now with the lawyer?"

Which gaffed me with an even sharper hook, since with Joanne sitting right beside her I couldn't tell Suzy even a fraction of the melange of half truths and whoppers I had served Keel. "Nothing serious," I said carelessly, and was hunting for my own exit from a trap when quite literally I was saved by the bell. The blast of the phone spelled salvation, and gratefully I stretched out a hand for the receiver. "Suite 810," I said into it.

"Zwack." Maybe it was a bad connection or a peculiarity of the man's telephone voice, but he didn't sound the same as he had before. "I'm downstairs. With some news I can't give you over the phone."

It was no time to drop security. "Quick," I said. "Name the director and star of *Too Many Winners.*"

"William Beaudine and Hugh Beaumont," he came back without a second's hesitation. "My, we're suspicious today! I didn't know thunderstorms brought out paranoia. Will you come down or do I come up?"

"Meet you in the coffee shop in five minutes," I said.

The waitress set a small bowl of fruit salad in front of Zwack's place in the high-backed green plush booth and a cup of black coffee at mine. The natty little gnome sprinkled bran atop the orange and grapefruit wedges, spooned up a bite, and sighed with satisfaction.

"So what's the uproar?" I asked him impatiently.

He waited till the mouthful went down before deigning to reply. "You wanted to know about any investigators that Jeffrey Haskell might have put on your lady's trail?"

"You found one?" My voice went a shade too high on the question.

"*If* you'll let me tell it my way." He smirked. "First of all, the agency that handles personnel checks and physical security for Haskell's Supermarkets is Sentry Associates. Their main office is in Clayton. One of the low-level paper-pushers fervently believes that she is worth more than Sentry pays her. In the spirit of economic equity I, er, supplement her salary now and then, mainly when I need confidential data from their files. I had her do a careful check. She assured me that at no time has Sentry been asked to look into the claim of any young woman that she was Bradford Haskell's daughter by his first marriage."

So Jeffrey was bluffing. For an awful moment I saw the whole Byzantine structure of my scam falling apart. My thoughts flew frantically in all directions at once as I tried to salvage something from the wreck.

Zwack cut into the silence. "Naturally I didn't stop there, not with you so certain that a detective had been hired. I started to work the problem from the other end." He stopped to refuel himself with a couple of spoonfuls of bran-laced fruit syrup. "Last night after business hours the Haskell Building had a visitor. A man with one of those cunning little Japanese cameras that fits in the palm of your hand. He photographed the pages of Jeffrey Haskell's daily appointment book for the entire period from the day your Ann Haskell arrived in Saint

Louis until the day she died. Thoroughness," he said proudly, "is our watchword."

"What did he find?" I demanded.

"At four thirty P.M. on Wednesday, April twenty-eighth, Haskell had a meeting scheduled with a Mr. Alan Ordway of Estates Investigative Services. Ever hear of that outfit?"

I shook my head no.

"It's a small organization based in Chicago. Founded four or five years ago by someone named Merton Grandell. They specialize in locating missing heirs, checking out claims against estates—that sort of work. This Ordway is billed as one of their senior fieldmen. You've never run into him before?"

"If there were a real Arthur Lattman he might have. Not me. Isn't he a PI like yourself?"

He made a face as if he'd bitten into a putrid grapefruit. "That animal is not the *least* like me! There's not an ounce of charm in him. He's broken legs for loan sharks, terrorized prospective witnesses in criminal trials until they refused to testify—all sorts of nasty stuff, according to the word I hear. There was never enough evidence against him for the state to yank his license. Then a few years ago he seemed to reform overnight. Went to work for Grandell at Estates Investigative Services and turned over a new leaf. If you like fairy tales."

My system seemed to know what was coming before the rest of me did. I could feel the rush of adrenaline. "Describe him," I said.

"I don't have to," he said. "A few more phone calls to connections in Chicago and I came up with this." He dropped his hand to the seat of the booth and handed me an unsealed manila envelope. I pulled out an 8½-by-11-inch photo, a glossy head and shoulders shot that looked professionally posed. Thin face. Dark haunted eyes that made his attempt to smile for the camera look pathetic. Scrawny neck, bony shoulders. He reminded me faintly of John Carradine the way he looked in *Stagecoach*. Except for the eyes and the way he wore his hair.

Combed straight back in a sharp widow's peak that looked like only one thing in the world. The letter *M*.

Bingo. A private peeper with a history of maiming people for money. The man who fit the description my lady had given me of the guy who was shadowing her in New York. I was holding between my fingers the image of her murderer. I wished to Christ it was his goddamn neck. But now I had him and Haskell both. That appointment book linked them together like a steel chain. I heard a singing roar like a waterfall in my head. I wanted to climb the coffee shop walls. *Cool it, fool, or you'll blow the works!*

Zwack kept chewing fruit salad as if he hadn't a care in the world, until I felt able to handle a conversation again.

"How are you fixed for people you can send to Chicago?" I asked him slowly, breathing deep to oxygenate the blood, calm me down.

"It's a slow season. I can send as many as you want."

"Get on Ordway's tail," I ordered. "Make sure he doesn't know he has company. Use six people if you have to."

"At two hundred dollars per person per day plus expenses?" He smiled shyly. "I suppose this is what they mean by carte blanche."

"Fuck the cost. Your tails won't be in Chicago long."

"And why not?"

"Because Ordway," I predicted, "will be back in Saint Louis very soon. And before he comes we're going to get ready for him."

Zwack wiggled a finger for the waitress and ordered a scoop of vanilla ice cream to which he added a liberal helping of bran, as we huddled together in the booth and talked security.

My own noon meal was consumed in suite 810, courtesy of room service and in the company of my wife and child after Zwack and I had nailed down the security plan and he had buzzed off. When lunch was over we went to the living room window and looked out at the new thunderstorm raging over the skyscape and decided without having to exchange words that the rest of the day had best be spent indoors. I switched on the TV and sampled an old Errol Flynn picture on one of the independent stations while Suzy took Joanne into the bedroom. Over the heroic declamations and cutlass-clanking from the tube I could hear the girl reading aloud from a book her mother had brought with her, a volume that by the conventional wisdom was several levels too difficult for a four-year-old. The sweet voice died away after a while, and Suzy came out of the room and deposited the book on an end table and dropped onto the couch beside me.

"She'll sleep for at least an hour," she said. "God, I love that little bug! . . . I knew you couldn't talk in front of her about that man you met in the coffee shop."

I jackknifed up and clicked off the set in the middle of a saber duel, came back to the couch and twisted around to face her. "Thanks for reading my body language so well. I did want to bring you up to date." I repeated what Zwack had told me, showed her the photo of Alan Ordway. "That's the man I'm after. Without being conspicuous about it I want you to watch for him everywhere you go from this minute on. He may start following us any time now."

Her jaw seemed to set with determination at the same time her pupils distended with the beginnings of fright. "I still can't believe that Jeffrey Haskell and his mousy little brother would hire an—an assassin to murder my child!"

"My dear," I said, "I've spent three months and close to a hundred thousand dollars to bait them into doing precisely that. I manipulated our meeting this morning to play games with their heads. They have to believe that Joanne's claim may be upheld in court *and also* that it may be a gigantic scam. That's why I deliberately oversold myself. It's why I hinted unnaturally soon that we'd be happy to settle out of court for less than a third."

A light seemed to snap on behind her hazel eyes. "*Now* I understand! You've been—well, recreating the situation that led up to—to the first murder."

"Exactly. Ann Haskell came here and made a plausible claim to a third of her father's residuary estate. Jeffrey suspected the claim might be a scam. He hired Ordway. Ann died in a perfectly timed accident, within less than a hundred twenty hours after Bradford Haskell's death. But keep in mind that when he paid Ordway to kill her, Jeff took a gamble—namely, that her claim would die with her. Now here comes a child with evidence that she's Ann's daughter, making the same claim Ann did. Once again Jeffrey suspects a scam. But if he does the natural thing and hires Ordway for another kill, he knows he's taking a much bigger gamble than the first time. Remember, Joanne has survived Bradford Haskell by a lot longer than one hundred twenty hours. Her rights in the estate have vested. If we're legitimate, her claim won't vanish even if all three of us die, it will just pass by will or intestate succession to others, probably distant relatives of Edward Blake, and all Jeffrey gains is a substitution of claimants. As a lawyer, Jeffrey knows this. It's only if we are fakes that Joanne's claim will die with her. That's why I've had to make us look both extremely plausible and at the same time subtly suspicious. I have to convince Jeffrey that we are con artists who've prepared so carefully that standard investigation will never touch us. If he believes that, he'll go to Ordway again, and I'll be ready and waiting for him."

Suzy's lower lip was trembling, as if she'd just realized that it wasn't a game she and her child were playing. "And you're certain he'll hire the same . . . the same hit man?"

"How many professional killers can a respectable corporate attorney know? Besides, the man gave complete satisfaction the first time."

"And you think he'll start shadowing us here in Saint Louis?"

"Keel will tell Haskell that we're going back to New York two weeks from today. I think they'd rather do the job here than back east. Cops in the same jurisdiction might get nasty ideas about two fatal accidents to Haskell legatees coming so close together. That's a lot less likely with the accidents being investigated in cities a thousand miles apart."

"Mr. Lattman," she said firmly, teeth tugging at her still trembling lower lip. "I told you that the minute I even suspected my child might be in danger, the two of us would walk out."

"I wouldn't think much of you if you didn't put Joanne's safety ahead of everything else. But will you let me try to convince you that there really isn't any risk?"

"You can try," she said, and her tone said that I wasn't terribly likely to succeed.

"All right. First, I've beefed up security around the hotel. You and Joanne won't be sleeping in this suite anymore, you'll slip out every night and take the fire stairs down to 709. The two of you will stay there with Sarah—that's the female half of the team that's protecting us inside the building. Her partner, Chuck, will take the fire stairs from 709 to this suite every night and stand watch here. Can Joanne be safer than that?"

"I—I guess not," she admitted hesitantly. "How about away from the hotel?"

"We'll have four people covering us wherever we go. That's a lot more than we need."

"You'd better explain that," she said, her eyes bright with calculation as she weighed risk factors.

"Remember, this Ordway isn't a lunatic or a political fanatic like the clowns that shot Reagan and the Pope. He's a paid killer, a businessman. He won't risk his life or freedom to take us out. That alone eliminates a lot of the danger. Then again, keep in mind that whatever he does has to look like an accident. He can't just wire a bomb to the ignition of the Cutlass. And since he can't know where we'll be or what we'll do from hour to hour he won't have a hell of a lot of opportunity to rig an accident."

"Even one opportunity is too many, Mr. Lattman," she said.

"You're right, of course. But look. Wherever we turn, we're going to be surrounded by bodyguards who will know exactly what this Ordway looks like. They're not going to wait for him to make an overt move. Once they see him, they grab him and you and Joanne can go back to New York."

"And what happens then?" she demanded.

"You really want to know?"

"Yes, Mr. Lattman, I do."

I had been rehearsing the next part in my daydreams, toying with it each night before I dropped off to sleep on the living room couch. "They turn him over to me," I said quietly. "I don't read him his Constitutional rights and I don't give him a lawyer. I do things to him you don't want to hear. When it's over, either he looks like something that would make Mother Teresa vomit or he signs a full confession implicating Jeffrey Haskell. Then I have to make two decisions."

She didn't ask the question but waited for me to go on.

"First, whether to finish the job on Ordway or turn him over to the law. Second, whether to leave Haskell to the law or settle with him personally too."

She sat there silently, eyes indrawn, and I knew I wasn't in the same world with her anymore. The decision she had to make was ripping her apart. I was afraid to move from my place on the couch, almost afraid to breathe. If I were in her shoes would I pull myself and my child out of the combat zone? And if that was what she did, what would I do then? I thrashed around in my head, playing with the idea of going to Chicago and connecting with a few bone-breakers who would help me snatch Ordway on his home turf and work on him till he spewed out a confession. Maybe it would be better that way. I wanted those sons-of-bitches more than anything in the world, but not at the expense of the woman and child I had recruited into this war. If anything happened to either of them I didn't think I could live with myself.

"What?" I shook myself like a water-splattered dog. My own internal dialogue had engrossed me so deeply I hadn't heard whatever she'd said.

"I said all right," she repeated, too loudly, with an undertone of anger at me and probably herself too. "For now, at least, we'll stay with you. But only on a one-day-at-a-time basis. The first hint of danger and we leave."

I let out a deep and relief-packed sigh and despised myself for it. "Deal," I said, and reached out for her hand. She drew it away and got up from the couch and crossed to the far corner of the room as if I were some kind of leper.

THIRTEEN

The hardest part of being a cop—so I was told once by several officers who were under the misapprehension that I was a journalist writing a laudatory article on law enforcement in their city—is the stakeout duty. The waiting for something to happen. Being keyed up for action and sitting out long nights in the cold and muck and then as often as not getting word from upstairs that the operation has been scrubbed. The consensus of those guys was that such work was more exhausting and more psychologically bruising than the rare moments of violence in the average cop's life.

They should try being a sacrificial goat sometime.

From the notebooks of Milo Turner

So we settled into our routine and waited for the man with the *M* on his head to try and kill us.

And nothing happened.

Edward P. Blake supposedly made his livelihood buying and restoring dilapidated houses and apartment buildings for resale later at a decent profit. It was an excellent cover story for a trip to Saint Louis, which has an abundant supply of solid old housing stock in urgent need of refurbishment. Several neighborhoods, like Hyde Park on the north side of the city and Soulard and Lafayette Square on the south, have enjoyed rehab booms, and property values there and in other locations have skyrocketed. I devoted a few prime hours every day to touring in the rented Cutlass, inspecting various structures seventy to a hundred years old that were for sale to potential rehabbers. Suzy and Joanne stuck close to the hotel and their guardians, swimming or reading or watching TV, and when they ventured afield it was always with a sizable tourist group. Every evening the three of us would go out to dinner: Schneithorst's when we felt like sauerbraten and potato pancakes, Abeyta's or Casa Gallardo for chicken mole and chimichangas and sopapillas, China Gardens for potstickers and pressed duck. Saint Louis County is crammed with gourmet eateries like these. We kept to the most popular spots where neither we nor our offstage attendants would stand out in the crowd.

Suzy was quiet and withdrawn those evenings, almost zombielike. It was as if she'd decided to cope with the situation by pretending it didn't exist, and the upshot was that both when we were in public and when we were alone we said hardly a word to each other. Probably made us look all the more like a typical married couple. Joanne on the other hand had so vague a notion of what was going on that she enjoyed herself immensely. The long lazy swimming lessons, the second visit to the zoo and to the Magic House in Kirkwood, and perhaps most delightful of all the new game of sneaking downstairs every night with her mother and sleeping in a different room, with a nice auntlike woman watching over their bed till morning.

That was the shape of our lives—until Sunday twilight, when the routine went haywire.

A little after nine Suzy and Joanne slipped out of 810 as usual, and two minutes later Sarah called up from 709 to let me know that my wife and child were tucked in for the night and all was well.

Only from my perspective it wasn't.

"What happened to Chuck?" I wanted to know. "He hasn't come up here yet."

"Oh, Christ," Sarah said softly. "He went out around six thirty, didn't say where. He should have been back half an hour ago. I thought he was with you."

"Call the office," I told her. "Get back to me soon as you learn anything." I hung up.

Suddenly I felt very much alone in that dim quiet suite. I felt like an escaping convict in one of those old prison movies, the guy who's cowering in the dark against a high wall and all of a sudden the whistles explode and the searchlight pins him and the machine guns start spitting at him. I hadn't packed a gun with me on this operation because I would have lost Suzy and Joanne for sure if they'd seen it, but as I walked the living room of 810 waiting for the phone to scream again I would have traded ten years of my life for a piece.

The phone went off. Scared me stone still for a few seconds. I ran across the room and caught it in the middle of the third ring. "Suite 810," I said as calmly as I could manage.

"C'est moi." It seemed to be the right voice and I couldn't imagine anyone trying to fake that playful lilt but was not in a mood to take chances.

"*Too Many Winners* was released when?" I demanded into the mouthpiece.

"Nineteen forty-seven, damn it!" he hissed. "Listen, we may have a problem. I had a call from Sarah a few minutes ago and one from the police shortly before that. Chuck is in the hospital. Someone mugged him in the Central West End a little after eight."

"Details," I said. "Snappy."

"He, ah, took a few hours off this evening on personal business. Probably to visit his girlfriend. In any event a black male in his late teens or early twenties conked him on the head and took his wristwatch and wallet."

"Then it wasn't Ordway."

"Not the man himself," Zwack agreed. "There's always

the possibility he's a progressive liberal and has a black associate, but it's most unlikely. How would they know Chuck was covering you? Why would they bother to put him out of action when he'd just be replaced by somebody else? Personally I would bet money that this has nothing to do with our case and is just one of those things that happen every day in the naked city."

"I don't know whether I hope you're right or not," I said. "He wasn't hurt badly?"

"They're keeping him in Barnes overnight for observation but he should be out in the morning. I'm going to take him off the case for a few days and send out another man to bodyguard you. He's on his way now and should be knocking on your door in half an hour or so."

"How will I know this man?"

"He'll know you. His name is Saltus Tebbs. He isn't a sprightly conversationalist and refuses to watch videocassettes with me after hours but he's a hell of a watchdog. Er . . . don't let his looks scare you. Night-night."

I hung up and went to the light switches and darkened the suite and slumped on the couch and waited and shivered. I don't know how much time passed. Ten minutes, maybe ten years. The noises from the outside corridor, sounds of ordinary men and women returning to their quiet caves after dinner, were filled with subtle menace.

The phone sounded again. I jerked up and caught it before the first ring died away. "Suite 810."

"Saltus Tebbs." It was a hulky uncultivated voice, hoarse and distorted as if the man had a bad case of laryngitis. "You want I should come up?"

"Do it," I said, and dropped the handset into the cradle.

I barely had time to get in position behind the seam of the suite's entrance door before the knock came. Just one knock that sounded like a thrown boulder. "Who is it?" I whispered.

"Tebbs," he growled. "Open the damn door."

I unchained it and as it flew open and formed a *V* I crouched in the seam with the wall against my back. In the light from the corridor I saw him backhand the door shut and swing around to face where I was. I cut my hand to the light switch beside the door and the floor lamp blazed into life over by the couch. When I took my first good look at what had barged in I almost had a heart attack.

He was about six six and weighed in the neighborhood of three hundred, and under a corn-colored wig that was second only to Harpo Marx's in implausibility he wore a face like the main attraction in a freak show. A tan bandage was stuck over the place where his right ear should have been. His nose looked sat-on. A knife scar made a jagged white trail from right eyebrow to jaw.

"You the guy I'm sposta baby-sit?" he whispered hoarsely.

The voice clinched it for me. We had never seen each other's faces before but six years ago we had had two close encounters, first in the Matchwit Club office and later outside an apartment building on First Avenue. And I had heard that sorry counterfeit of a human voice during a brief phone conversation for which I had borrowed another man's sound. Today he was calling himself Saltus Tebbs, but the last time our worlds had converged his name had been Moose Eliot.

That was one of the least restful evenings of my life. Keeping a poker face all through the small talk and routine of buttoning up suite 810 for the night, I had to question my own sanity as I locked myself in with a mush-brained man mountain equipped with the brute force of a rogue bull elephant and a .38 automatic for good measure. If he picked up even a hint that we had once been on opposite sides of an extremely high fence, I was dead. Frantically I resurrected every fragment of memory from the Matchwit operation. Was there a split second when he'd seen me in the back rooms of the club? No. He was just coming out of the john when I slipped through the door in the wall that opened on the main supper room, and in any event I'd been wearing a hairpiece that was of infinitely better quality than his own. Could he have seen me outside the First Avenue building? No way, I'd been hidden around the corner and he'd had his back to me all the time until he climbed into the taxi. So the bottom line was that I knew a hell of a lot about him and he knew nothing about me except that I was a client of Eagle Eye who was paying for an inordinate amount of protection. Even if Zwack had been so indiscreet as to let slip to the hired hands that they were watching over the incomparable Milo Turner—and I had expressly ordered him to keep that tidbit to himself—the information wouldn't mean anything special to the Moose or Saltus or whatever his name was, because there was no way he could know that Milo T. was the man who had knocked over Max Gantry's laundry. But I couldn't help being curious about the way life had treated this hulk during the intervening six years, and I thrashed around for some device that would open him up and start him talking without exposing my own skin.

As things turned out, my wish was granted without effort on my part. With Tebbs as my bodyguard and no chance of scaring up yet another substitute from Zwack I abandoned all hope of a sound night's sleep and plugged in the portable coffee maker I had bought on my first day in Saint Louis and brewed an extra-strong potful. I filled a pair of plastic cups and, ever mindful of a host's obligations, carried one of them to the chair where Tebbs had draped himself with his back against one arm and his tree-trunk legs across the top of the other and the .38 in his lap.

"Thanks," he grunted, making no move to reach for the cup. "Never touch the stuff."

"Suppose I put something in to cool it down?"

"Now, that's hospitality!" He bared ruined teeth in an innocent childlike grin.

I rummaged in my suitcase in the front closet and unearthed the fifth of Wild Turkey, which was the only liquor I had allowed myself to buy during the operation, and sweetened his coffee with a splash of the stuff, a light one, since after all he was supposed to be my protector. He downed it in one gulp, belched, lurched out of the chair and over to the coffee maker and refilled his cup and to the bottle and poured. By midnight the fifth was dead, and the only effect it seemed to have had on him was to put him in a mellow inquisitive mood. He started to pump me about what we were after on this operation. I told him what he perfectly well knew already, that it was a trap for a hit man whose hair grew in a widow's peak shaped like the letter M. He wanted to know why I was out for this hit man. In my most laconic style I replied that he had wasted the wrong person. Then he began asking questions about who I was. At first I was tempted to stop yakking with him and try to sleep, but after a few minutes' reflection I saw the strategic value of opening the biographical floodgates and spun for my guardian angel a labyrinth of lies which he was just soused enough to accept. An hour later I tapered off the flow of spontaneous oral invention and, with the subtlety of a chess master maneuvering his opponent into the Fool's Mate, switched the subject to Tebb's own curriculum vitae.

It worked.

" . . . I came out here and hooked up with Zwack, oh,

three, maybe four years back. He uses me when he hasta throw a real scare into somebody. Resta the time I drive guys around, clean up the office, stuff like that. Zwack don't trust the building janitors."

"Keeping a low profile, huh?"

"You look at the profeel, you see why." He cackled grimly at the mention of his horror-show face.

"Bet there's a hell of a story in how that happened to you," I said casually. "You don't want to talk about it, I guess."

"It don't bother me. I never was no Paul Newman even before." Another cackle. "I got this kisser back in Noo Yawk when I was a sort of bouncer and gofer for a bastard named Max Gantry. I came to work for him— let's see, early in seventy-six it was. He and some old fart were partners in this place they called the Matchwit Club, and the old fart kicked off and Gantry was running the whole show when he took me on. He had a lot of private business on the side, use ta keep mucho cash in a secret safe in the club office—sometimes thirty, thirty-five thou. Some babe he was sleeping with sent some other guy she was fucking around with to try and open the safe. Gantry caught on the chick was screwing him over, and he and I paid her a visit."

I was doing a rotten job of keeping the emotion off my face, but he was too full of sauce and his own memories to notice. "You killed her?" Oh so disinterestedly I asked the question.

"Just messed her up a little. Gantry broke a few of her fingers with a hammer and she was real happy to give us the boyfriend's address. Gantry left me with the chick and went to settle with the guy, but the guy outfoxed him and left him trussed up and with his puss mashed in. Then, as good as I can figure out what happened, the guy made a phone call to where I was with the broad and pretended he was Gantry and told me to beat it back to the club, the cops was coming. So I went and he got the chick and took off."

"You didn't go after them?"

"Things didn't break that way. Gantry went crazy. He blamed me for letting both of them get free. Hell, I wasn't even around when the guy beat up on him, but Gantry always found someone else to blame when anything went wrong. Anyway, he put four or five strong-arm men on me and they took me out to the woods someplace and Gantry woiked on me with a knife. They left me for dead out there, threw me on top of a pile of animal shit. Well, I wasn't dead, but I wished to Christ I was for a while there. . . . You wanna hear how I got patched up?"

Actually I had but the mildest interest in that topic, but it held no emotional threat for me so I invited him to go on. It was a rambling account that took the better part of an hour. The only segment to which I paid full attention dealt with when he was well enough to start savoring the prospect of taking his own knife to the face of Max Gantry.

" '. . . And the hell of it was I was six months too late. His wop pals saved me the trouble."

"The same ones you said he had some private business with?"

"That was the woid I hoid. This sideline got hit by an outside operator and the big boys lost like a million bucks. Well, you lose that kinda dough you lean on someone, and they leaned on Gantry. I wasn't there to see what they done to him but I bet they took their sweet time and made him sorry he was born, you know?"

"Yeah," I said softly.

"No one ever found what they left of him," he said. "He just went up in smoke like Jimmy Hoffa. So anyway, man, I know how you feel about evening scores and I hope you're luckier than me and get to do it yourself."

At this point the digital clock on top of the TV was reading 2:07 and my own modest indulgence in the Wild Turkey caught up with me. I fell onto the couch and kicked off my shoes and socks and suddenly remembered and lumbered to my feet and padded across to the TV and set the digital alarm for 7:30 so I could be up and about and hustle Saltus out of the joint before my child came in and was scared half to death.

I dreamed of my lady drawing a convolution of invisible lines on my naked belly and talking about the weird patterns life makes.

It was a far from rested Milo who tooled the Cutlass into downtown Saint Louis late the next morning and miraculously found a vacant parking meter on Olive Street and fed a quarter into the slot and marched into the Parkway Building. The Eagle Eye Investigations receptionist seemed to recognize me as the client of the month and ushered me deferentially into the honcho's sanctum. Zwack, in a beige suit that would have been considered mod in the late sixties, sat erect behind his desk studying a pamphlet, which he held out to me as I sank into the visitor's chair.

"I can't make up my mind," he greeted me. "This dealer has videocassettes of selected episodes from some of the earliest private eye TV series like *The Cases of Eddie Drake* and *The Files of Jeffrey Jones* but I think his prices are way out of line. What should I do?"

"Wait till they show up on cable and tape them yourself," I said. "You're not too busy to have a little conference with me, I trust?"

"Why, my dear sir, our world revolves around you!" He beamed like a starving artist at an unexpected visit from his patron and shoved the videotape catalogue into a drawer. "How can I be of service?"

"For starters you can fill me in on what's happened

with the people you were supposed to send to Chicago after Ordway."

"I was afraid it might be that." He allowed his eyelashes to flutter dramatically. "I didn't want to report till I was sure, but Ordway seems to have vanished from his usual haunts."

"When?"

"Around the time of your session with the Haskell family last week. Perhaps a day or two later."

"That means he's had a hell of a long time to set things up in Saint Louis," I pointed out. "Are you certain none of your people have spotted him?"

"Absolutely. And each of them has his own print of Ordway's picture."

"Okay," I said. "That's what we've messed up. Give me a copy of that photo."

Zwack opened the shallow center drawer of his desk and extracted a glossy print, which he set down neatly on the blotter.

"What's the most conspicuous thing about the man?" I demanded.

"We-e-ell, his hairline is so . . . Nixonian. It reminds me of that magnificent scene in Fritz Lang's *M* when the beggar drew the letter in chalk on the back of the psychotic's jacket."

"If you were a professional hit man would you go around with a hairline like that?"

"Not unless I was subconsciously trying to be caught, like Peter Lorre in *M*. I don't think Mr. Ordway falls into that category."

"My point exactly. He doesn't feel threatened by that hairline. Deduction: he doesn't use it on a job. Either he covers it with a wig or maybe the *M* hairline is phony itself. If your men have been watching for the hairline and not the man they've been playing into his hands."

"Oh, my." Zwack clucked mildly. "Suddenly all sorts

of possibilities confront us. I, er, can't guarantee that all of my people would be able to recognize him just from his general facial cast."

"Then let's help them out," I said. "Get hold of one of those Identikits the cops use. Have an artist draw as many variants of the basic face as possible. Some with beards, some without, some with mustaches, some without. Every kind of hairline he can imagine."

"On short notice all this will cost a few dollars," he murmured.

"God damn it, this is not a game! Do it!"

"Right away," he said. "But may I ask what started you thinking along these, ha ha, lines?"

"Saltus Tebbs's lousy wig," I told him.

The more I thought about it the shakier it made me. Before I left the Eagle Eye office I made Zwack agree to drop everything else, call in his off-shift people, and have them study Identikit variations of Ordway's face. He promised to call if he got results.

As I sped west on I-70 back to the Centurion Inn, paranoia hit me between the eyes and I almost let go the steering wheel of the Cutlass. We had no idea where Ordway was and only the vaguest fix on what he looked like. He was tall, with mournful eyes and a turkey neck and thin shoulders, but contact lenses and padding could change most of that. He might be any tall man in any crowd of tourists in Saint Louis. He could have been in the same elevator car with Suzy and Joanne and me when we rode to the observation platform atop the arch, or behind us on the deck of the *Samuel Clemens* when we took the boat tour of the riverfront. I had sudden visions of him pushing that child down one of the arch's service staircases, lifting her over the deck rail, and tossing her into the Mississippi. I floored the gas pedal, saw the red speedometer needle inch past seventy, and the hotel still seemed a hundred miles away.

I raced across the parking lot and the lobby and into a cage and out at eight and twisted my key in the knob slot of 810. It wouldn't turn. Dead bolt must be on. I pounded on the door. Come on, damn it, *come on*! Slap of steps across the living room. Sound of the chain lock being undone. I choked the knob and went in and reset the dead bolt and chain behind me.

Suzy by the door and Joanne halfway across the room wore their matching beach robes over bathing suits that were still wet. They must have come up from a dip in the pool just a minute before I banged on the door.

"Do not leave this room till I say you can." I kept the command low so the child couldn't hear. "Order your meals from room service. Don't let Joanne out of your sight. Understand?"

Her eyes went bulgy and she gave a quick gasp that was just loud and sharp enough to cut through my paranoid mood and make me see that I was terrifying her. "Sorry," I said idiotically. "There really isn't anything wrong. Just an insecurity spasm." I should have kept my big trap shut. She wheeled around, took Joanne by the hand, and led her into the bedroom. When she came out she eased the door shut and crossed to where I stood by the long low couch and looked into my eyes with a grim determination that scared me the way a minute ago I had shaken her.

"I told you what I would do," she said fiercely, "if I even suspected my child was at risk. Now, do you pick up that phone and make two reservations on the next flight to New York or do I?"

I didn't try to argue with her because I knew she was right. I had invested three months and close to a hundred thousand dollars in digging a trap and making the bait irresistible, but an hour of irrational conviction that tne tiger was skulking in the underbrush had torn the scam to shreds and now I would have given everything I had to protect the bait that had become so precious to me.

"Game's over," I said lightly. "No score." I stumbled to the phone and punched first the 9 for an outside connection and then the airline's number. A recorded message put me on hold and canned music drifted over the line. I cursed under my breath and began to count and was nearing forty when a live voice greeted me. I explained what I wanted and the voice put me on hold and I fought the urge to bang down the handset and scream. The voice came back with information in excruciating detail. I set the receiver down and gave a quick summary to Suzy.

"This is the busiest month of the tourist season. They don't have two seats together till the nine fifty flight this evening."

"Take them," she told me. "I want us out of this place." I lifted the handset and made the reservations and recited the numbers of Edward P. Blake's MasterCard into the mouthpiece and thanked the voice and hung up.

The phone call had eased some of the tension lines around Suzy's eyes and mouth. "Thank you," she said simply. "I know how much catching this man means to you."

"Not as much as your safety and Joanne's. I'll get him another way."

"Luck," she said, and came over to me and kissed me on the cheek. I reached out for her, held her against me and breathed the soft scent of her hair. She didn't move away. My hands tightened their grip at her waist and her mouth sought mine and her arms locked around my neck and what began as a cool tentative playful kiss built and grew into frenzy and desperation. I explored the sweetness of her mouth and caressed her tanned neck and shoulders, but when I tried to fumble with the fastening of her maillot she tugged my fingers away and nodded almost with terror toward the bedroom door behind which Joanne was waiting.

"Any chance Sarah's still downstairs?" she whispered into my ear.

I let her go and bent to the phone and punched 709 and counted rings. *Oh, please be in the room.* I wasn't worried about Ordway anymore. Suddenly he was on a distant planet.

"Yes?"

The world was good to me that day: it was Sarah's voice. Without explaining I asked if she'd mind sitting with Joanne for a couple of hours. She said it would be a pleasure. I thanked her too profusely and lowered the handset and made a *V* sign with my fingers. Suzy smoothed her beach robe and went into the bedroom and came out in less than a minute with Joanne. I waited in the doorway of 810, watched them vanish into the fire tower. Her steps came slapping up the stairs again in a half run. We locked, chained, and bolted the door.

"Think Sarah knows?"

"If she's any sort of a detective she guessed." Suzy shrugged off her robe and let it fall in a heap on the floor and fumbled at the back of her neck for the fastening of her swimsuit. She let it drop to her waist and reached out for me and drew my lips to her proud firm breasts that were still moist from the pool and she moaned as the pink nipples came alive in my mouth. I heard my blood pounding. We never made it as far as the bedroom.

Later, with passion momentarily spent, we lay entangled on the couch making little noises of contentment, each of us waiting for the other to initiate a new episode. She ran her pale pointed nails along my chest. "Come back with us tonight," she said. "I know someone I can leave Joanne with. We'll open up the apartment in Astoria. I want you to see some paintings I've done of myself that I've never shown anyone before."

"What kind of paintings?"

"Oils. A few watercolors."

"You know what I meant, clown."

"You know what kind of paintings, tease."

"They'll never turn me on like you do in the flesh," I said, and we reached for each other again. That long lazy afternoon our pent-up physical needs exploded like thunderclaps. I hadn't been with a woman since that night almost three months ago, and the way Suzy responded, the way she would literally purr like a cat after climax, told me that for her it had been a hell of a lot longer than that.

I was caressing her all over, and almost ready to scrub the scam, cut my losses, and count myself well ahead and catch the owl flight back east with her, when the phone went off again.

Suzy sighed. "Let it be, love."

"It might be Sarah about Joanne," I reminded her, and reluctantly disengaged myself and caught it on the fifth ring. "Suite 810."

"Lucky I found you in." The voice was Zwack's but sans all the cutesy mannerisms. "I just finished talking to the people I've had watching the hotel. Looks like you have a problem."

I waited. There was no sense alarming Suzy by asking what kind of problem, at least not yet. One of those prophetic voices that live in my skull warned me that there would soon be enough fear for both of us.

"Two of the men are ninety percent certain they saw Ordway with a different head of hair hanging around the Centurion yesterday and this morning. The most reliable fellow on my staff says he'd stake his life it was

Ordway. Between the three of them they came up with an excellent picture of what he looks like at the moment. Will you be in your room for a while?"

"Why?"

"We-e-ell, the assistant manager out there owes me a favor. I'm leaving for the hotel right now with a copy of our sketch that he can show to the check-in personnel. If the man is registered there you will want to know right away, I assume."

"Good thinking," I said. "Buzz when you have something." I hung up and turned back to Suzy who was shrugging on her long-ago discarded beach robe.

"You'd better get dressed and go downstairs with Joanne and Sarah," I told her. "And stay there till you hear from me, okay?"

"He's here," she said softly. A pulse jumped in her temple.

"He may be here," I corrected her. "With luck we'll know for sure in an hour or two. Whatever happens, I want you and Joanne safe."

"I know you do," she said.

I kissed her at the front door and saw her as far as the fire stairs landing and buttoned myself up in 810 again and called 709 to make sure all was well. After that I had nothing to do but wait. Well, almost nothing. As a precaution and to keep the dead time from pushing me off the deep end I spent the next hour packing our suitcases. First mine, then, with what fastidiousness I could muster in the circumstances, Suzy's and Joanne's. I lugged the bags into the front closet and checked the suite to make sure I hadn't missed anything. The digital clock on the TV read 3:47. I dropped into an armchair and tried to empty my mind and relax and felt my insides tightening.

The wait lasted forever by my own mental time and about twenty minutes by the digital. I heard a staccato rap on the door and jerked like a frog's leg in the old high school electricity experiment and edged over to the front hall. "Yes?" I meant it to sound sharp and decisive but it came out thin and quavery.

"Zwack. Let me in!" he demanded.

"Not till you give me the names of those TV series on cassette we were talking about this morning."

"Oh, for Christ's sake! *The Cases of Eddie Drake* and *The Files of Jeffrey Jones.*"

I undid the locks and let him in and secured the place again.

"He's in the hotel," Zwack reported. "He and a woman registered early yesterday afternoon as Mr. and Mrs. Kenneth Holland of Chicago."

"Any description of the woman?"

"Tall, thin, somewhere in her thirties. Nothing we can identify her by."

"What room are they in?"

"They are a couple with special needs. Not too high nor too low, away from the elevator noise and near an exit. The registration clerk put them in 906."

"One flight up and just a few doors down the hall from the fire stairs. How long are they supposed to be staying?"

"The form they made out says three nights."

"And they've already been here more than twenty-four hours," I said, "and nothing's happened."

"We-e-ell, they need time to case the building, work out the most plausible accident."

"Oh, Jesus," I said. "Suzy and Joanne were in the pool this morning! Ordway could have been paddling around right behind them, waiting to get the kid alone and hold her head under." Suddenly and in spite of all my elaborate security arrangements I hated myself for putting that woman and child at the slightest risk. I felt my eyes blinking uncontrollably, a nervous twitch that serves as my conscience.

Zwack tried to argue me out of the guilt sulk. "There is no chance he could have caught the child alone in an Olympic-size hotel pool on an August day in Saint Louis. By now he's surely devised a better plan than that."

Plan, plan, what was his plan? If I were Ordway and had to kill a child in a strange city and the murder had to pass as an accident, how would I do it? Would I bank on my ability to anticipate the family's movements, separate the child from her parents in a public place, and rig an accident? If not, would I gamble on killing all three of them in a public place and an apparently accidental manner? Not if I had a better option I wouldn't. And why did I need a room so close to theirs?

It was as if I had slumped into a trance. I could see Zwack staring bug-eyed at me from the matching arm-chair, but he was no more real to me than an image on a screen. I was in a universe where no one could keep me company. For the first time since this bloody mess had begun I was thinking like Milo, son of the King Fox.

After God knows how long a journey through inner space I shook my head like a punch-drunk pug and snapped back to the public world.

"I know what he's going to do," I said, "and I think I know when."

Zwack was still gaping at me and clearly incapable of dialogue. I had mercy on him and took him off the hook at once.

"It's tonight," I said.

FOURTEEN

All you have to do to compose a symphony is to make your selections from the infinity of possible sounds and organize them into a structure such that, hearing the final movement, the listener will catch its echoes in what came before and give a tiny gasp of recognition and satisfaction. All you have to do to write a novel is to select from the infinity of words and order them so that at the climax the reader will catch the echoes from earlier chapters and give the same sort of gasp. Creating something aesthetically inevitable is simplicity itself. After all, isn't the world full of people like Beethoven and Shostakovich and Dickens?

The only talent it takes is the ability to imitate life.

From the notebooks of Milo Turner

Without exposure to critical thinking, intuition isn't worth shit. For the balance of that long afternoon we sat on the edges of the matching armchairs thoughtfully provided by the Centurion Inn and role-played. Zwack's part was the devil's advocate. Erect as a private sitting in the colonel's office, he raised every objection imaginable to my hunch or mystical precognition or whatever you want to label the way I knew Ordway's next move. Our dialogue had precisely the effect I was hoping for. It made him believe more fervently than I did myself.

But he still had problems with where my certainty had come from. Or as he put it, "My God, man, how can you reach like that into the mind of someone you've never even seen?"

"Nothing occult about it," I assured him. "But it helps if you've spent years being other people and seeing the world as they do. Put yourself in Ordway's shoes. He has to kill the child, and Suzy and me too, in a way that will pass as an accident. He wants to do it here in Saint Louis because that way there's only minimal risk that our deaths will be connected with the accidental death of another Haskell family member in New York three months ago. That means he has to do it soon. If you want confirmation of that point, remember he rented 906 only for three nights. Now, what kind of accident can be arranged quickly that would fit in with our life-style on this Saint Louis trip? *A hotel fire.* You read the papers, there's been a rash of those infernos lately. What better way to wipe out a family of three without raising suspicions? That's why he maneuvered to get a room near the fire stairs and close to this suite, and it's also the reason he brought a woman or a disguised man with him. One person can't do all the work. And they've already had twenty-four hours to reconnoiter, so I think it's going to happen tonight."

"Let me hear your version of their strategy again," Zwack said.

"Gladly. I am Ordway, planning to torch the hotel tonight. My first order of business is to break into this suite somehow, hold the Blakes at gunpoint, stun them so the marks won't show, and fix the props so it looks like they couldn't get out in time and died of smoke inhalation. When that part's done, my buddy and I go out in the hall and set fire to something, maybe one of the window drapes at the end of the corridor. Then we shoot back up to 906 and put on our nightshirts and make like terrified hotel guests. In a few minutes the building's a madhouse, smoke and flames and fire alarms and people screaming and pouring out of their rooms. If some of them die in the fire, too, so much the better, it looks more like an accident that way. Who'd believe a killer would burn down a huge hotel just to waste one little girl?"

"I still can't accept it," he growled impotently, "but you've convinced me of one thing. The time has come for an anonymous phone call to the Saint Louis County Police."

"No!" I almost shrieked the word. "No cops, God damn it! This is between Ordway and me."

"Turner, I will not risk the lives of the people in this building just so you and these clowns can have a private duel." He lifted himself out of his chair and took a few steps toward the door.

"There is no risk." I caught him halfway across the room and spun him around by the shoulder. "Please," I begged him. "Just give me ten minutes to show you they won't even come close to lighting the match. Not if we do this my way."

He didn't wax ecstatic over the proposal but in the end he agreed to go along with me. And so as happy hour came and went and dinnertime merged into early twilight, we generals prepared for the last battle.

First priority was getting a fix on the enemy position. We rang 906 half a dozen times in ten minutes without response. "I figured they'd go out to dinner somewhere," I said, "They know we'll be sleeping here tonight, because if we were going to check out we'd have done it early this afternoon and saved a night's charges. They couldn't care less where we go or what we do until bedtime, so there's no reason why they shouldn't enjoy a gourmet meal."

"*Bon appétit* to them both," Zwack said. "They're giving me the opportunity to hang ears on them while they're away."

"You mean bug their room?"

"Too risky. No, I shall simply trot down to the lobby and check into this delightful establishment, using my wiles to get assigned something as close to 906 as possible." He wafted out of the armchair and made for the front door. "Call you soon."

Eight minutes later I caught the phone at the first instant it exploded into noise. "Suite 810."

"Do you believe in the power of prayer? Or lucky stars? Or in good luck amulets perhaps? Anyway, 905 was vacant, and at this moment there is nothing but a wall between their base and me. I've already called the office. Three men and some equipment are on their way."

"Looking good," I said. "Ordway's not back from dinner yet?"

"I don't hear any sounds from next door."

"Then let's get Suzy and Joanne out of here. They're still with Sarah and Chuck in 709."

"Right. I'll have my pair check out with all the ladies' luggage. When my men deliver the equipment I'll have one of them check into another room on seven. He can then walk out of the hotel with the Misses French on his arm like his own wife and child. We'll keep them downtown at the office till it's time to drive them to Lambert for their New York flight."

"Sounds fine," I said. "Now remember, some time tonight Ordway and his partner are going to leave 906 and take the fire stairs down here. You have to get word to me the minute they're out the door."

"That's what the equipment I ordered is for. But do you really think they're counting on your being naive enough to open for them in the middle of the night?"

"They'll find a way of making me want to let them in," I predicted. "That's the easiest part of the operation for them. Just give me all the early warning you can, okay?"

"If they give even the slightest sign that they're going to go about this ass backward and set the fire before they get into your room—"

"Then you have my permission to blow them into little pieces," I said.

Night closing down around a high-rise airport hotel. The muffled roars as planes take off or come in become fewer and are separated by longer silences as the flights thin out. Your concentration centers on the noises in the corridor. Organizes the footsteps and voices into pictures. Men coming back from dinner, a meeting, a show, a bar, talking about the business they had transacted today or would transact in the morning. Women coming back from the same kinds of places, talking about relationships, their own or others'. A man and a women returning together, whispering. Mechanical snick of elevator door opening or closing. Bang of room doors. Distant buzz of television as the guests of the Centurion Inn prepared for bed to the rhythm of Johnny Carson's monologue or the black humor of *M*A*S*H*. Explosion of toilet flush. Roar of shower water. And as night wore on the noise level dropped. The only people coming along the corridor now were the types who closed the bars, and they made their way from elevator to room either quarrelsomely or merrily or in the silence of despair, depending on how the booze affected them. At the edge of sound I could make out the noises that, when you are without a partner of your own, can rip you in half with loneliness. I sat in the lotus position on the carpet in the front hallway of 810, cataloguing all the noises, straining for the sounds that would mean they were coming to kill me.

In the empty hours after midnight, with Suzy and Joanne in the air and most of the way to New York, doubts crept into the echoing cave I called my mind.

Maybe, just maybe, there was no menace out there at all. Suppose the man who had checked into 906 was a guy named Kenneth Holland who had some vague resemblance to Alan Ordway but no connection in the world with that butcher. Suppose Ordway himself wasn't the man who'd been shadowing my lady in New York but just looked a bit like him: a lot of men have *M*-shaped hairlines. It was even possible that the New York shadow was another innocent bystander, a creep dreaming of picking my lady up but afraid to make his move: thousands of men are terrified of rejection by a woman. In the whole long sequence of events that had brought me to this room there was hardly a happening that couldn't be written off as coincidence. After all, bigger coincidences than these had already taken place in the story. Look at the way the second Ann Haskell and I had met in front of the bar on Fifty-seventh Street. Look at how Moose Eliot from the Matchwit Club had popped into the Saint Louis end of the operation as Saltus Tebbs. It was possible that everything I'd done and all the expense of time and sweat and money was a laughable waste, that I'd been following a false trail devised by chance.

What fits better with the world we know, the notion that everything just sort of happens or that a malignant god out there is toying with us? Tonight I was betting on the god. If I was right, he would make his appearance before sunrise and I would stamp him out. If I was wrong—and as the black hours crept I came to be more and more afraid that I was—I'd have to return to square one, start life over again somehow, never knowing how or why my lady had died.

So I sat like Buddha on the floor and listened to the hotel's night noises and waited and almost prayed for the coming. The walkie-talkie phone Zwack had left with me was resting on the carpet where I could scoop it up in a wink, and all the reinforcement a man could need was snoring blissfully just out of sight. Even without a gun of my own I felt halfway secure.

Until the cordless phone made its tweety-bird sound and turned my spine into a chilled steel tube. My watch showed six to midnight. I snatched up the talk box, scuttled out of the hallway into the living room, and whispered into the mouthpiece. "What's up?"

"They came back ten minutes ago." Zwack kept his voice low, cool, and free of melodrama. "I can hear them talking in 906 but I can't pick up a word, the damn spike mike's on the blink."

"A man and a woman?"

"Two men. Either Mrs. Kenneth Holland was a man in drag or else she's an accomplice who checked in with Ordway to make them look like an ordinary couple and then let the male partner take over. Now, would you like to hear something really fascinating about the second man?"

"Watchful waiting bores the shit out of me. Go on, fascinate me."

"I've had a woman operative in the cocktail lounge that forms part of the lobby area downstairs. She saw Ordway and the other man come in ten minutes ago and phoned me up here. Now, as it happens, this young lady has an incredible memory for faces and is also, we-e-ell, a lot of fun at conventions. I took her with me last year to a PI conference in Honolulu. And she swears that she met Ordway's partner at that conference. You know who she says the man is?"

"Dr. Mengele, the death angel of Auschwitz," I guessed.

"Merton Grandell," he said. "The CEO of Estates Investigative Services. Ordway's boss. As the immortal Poirot used to say, it gives one furiously to think, *n'est-ce pas*?"

He clicked off and left me alone in the night to chew on his information. I began to toy with the theory that

Estates Investigative Services might be a cover for professional killers. That was when my creative juices burst their banks. My God, what a specialty! Suppose Grandell's real business was not finding missing heirs but arranging accidental deaths so as to increase his customer's share of some estate? Posit a dying millionaire with three children who know that they take equally under his will. Given the right family circumstances, if A hires Grandell to waste B or C before the old bird dies, A's share will climb from a third to a half. And in case the tycoon dies too soon and B or C, the intended victim, is still alive, if Grandell can accidentally dispose of him within one hundred twenty hours the same result might still be reached, provided of course that the victim left no descendants.

All of a sudden a wild desire seized me. I didn't want to be staked out in this hotel room like a sacrificial goat. I wanted to be in Chicago, breaking into Grandell's files, finding out how many contacts he'd had with wealthy families in which an accidental death of some sort had redistributed the survivors' shares of a large estate. Maybe I could do that tomorrow.

The adrenaline was racing through me now, strong as white water. I was keyed up for action, tensed for another birdcall from the walk-phone. The minutes crawled. The hotel was tomb quiet, everyone wrapped in a private cocoon. Almost everyone.

Tweetweetweet. My watch read 12:42. I lifted the box to my ear and mouth. "Nine oh six is dead," Zwack reported. "They're in bed. You know, this may not be the night after all."

"They won't move till the building's asleep. Meanwhile they're professionals and will nap while they can. Keep listening." I clicked off, went over to the couch, and allowed myself the ineffable luxury of stretching out with my head propped up on one of its arms and my feet draped over the other, the walk-phone balanced two inches from my ear so it would wake me in an instant in case I could bring down my nerves from their screaming high alert and sink into a cozy little nap of my own. Realistically I didn't think I could rest for a minute.

The *tweetweetweet* jerked me awake. I grabbed the box. My watch read 2:36. Jesus, I'd been out like a light for the better part of two hours!

"The alarm in 906 went off ten minutes ago," Zwack said softly. "They're moving around. I think they . . . wait a minute, I just heard their door quietly closing. They're out in the corridor."

Sweat trickled down my back and sides. "Heading for the fire stairs?"

"The other way, toward the elevators. Get ready."

I stuck the walk-phone under one of the armchairs and paced the living room carpet, my nerves screaming again. Any moment now I might hear the soft insistent tapping at the front door. No, I decided. They were headed for the elevator, not the fire stairs, so they probably were going to call from the lobby, set me up to let them in. I braced for the shock of hearing the explosion a phone makes in the middle of the night when you are alone in the dark.

When it came I leapt into the air like Nijinsky.

Edward P. Blake was supposed to be sound asleep in the bosom of his family. He wouldn't answer on the first ring. How long would it take him to stumble out of bed and catch it? Four rings? Five? I gave him five. Made myself endure those howls of phone noise. On five I picked up. "Suite 810," I muttered in a half awake and thoroughly annoyed tone. "What the hell . . . ?"

"Mr. Edward Blake?"

I knew that voice. It pierced my memory like a hot spike, but at that moment and under those circumstances I couldn't fit a name to it. Then I had it. I knew whom that low hypnotic voice belonged to but I still couldn't believe it. For one awful moment I was afraid I'd gone over the edge, joined the brotherhood of those who make their own reality.

"Who is this?" I kept the anger and sleepiness in my voice and fought to control the racing of my thoughts and blood.

"This is Mr. Gordon downstairs, the night manager, sir. I'm terribly sorry to disturb you at this hour, Mr. Blake, but is the car you're driving a black nineteen eighty-one Cutlass, license number CCS-472?"

"Yes, that's the car we rented."

"Your, er, wife and child wouldn't be out driving in it at this hour, would they, sir?"

"Suzy and Joanne are here with me," I said. "Sleeping. Or at least they were until you woke them. Mr. Gordon, what the hell is going on down there?"

"Mr. Blake, I have some bad news for you. It seems that someone broke into your car in the parking lot and drove off with it. A short while ago it was involved in a serious accident on I-270. Sergeant Leslie from the state highway patrol is here with me. He needs to come up and ask you a few questions."

I seasoned my reply with the proper tones of shock and disbelief. "Oh my God, was anyone hurt badly? . . . Yes, of course I'll speak to him."

A new voice came on at the other end, one that I decided had to be Alan Ordway. "Mr. Blake, this is Sergeant Leslie. It won't take long, but there are some questions I have to ask you immediately."

"Give me two minutes, I'll put on some clothes and come right down." That was to test him. If I read the situation right he'd veto my suggestion and insist on seeing me in the suite.

He did. "No, sir," he said quickly. "I'll have to ask

your wife a few questions too. I'll be at your door in a minute."

"All right," I said, and hung up.

This was zero hour. They had made that call from a booth or house phone in the lobby. Now they'd come up in the elevator and like a cooperative little citizen I would open the door of 810 for them. That was their scenario. Probably Ordway had used a similar trick to get into the New York apartment rented in Ann Haskell's name. I trotted into the bedroom to make sure that the reception I'd prepared was ready, then back into the living room to wait. Objectively it couldn't have taken more than a minute, but to my own time sense it seemed that the Mahler Ninth Symphony could have been performed in the interval between the breaking of the phone connection and the sharp snick of the elevator door opening and closing at the far end of the hall. I heard steps shuffling along the carpeted hallway, then even that soft sound died. They must be right in front of 810 now. There was a sharp urgent KGB nighttime rap on the door.

Edward P. Blake was supposed to be expecting a visitor. I allowed only a few seconds before I went to the door and whispered, "Yes?"

"Sergeant Leslie, sir."

"Just a minute, please." I made a production number out of undoing the dead bolt and chain and twisting the knob, but the show ended abruptly when the door flew open and revealed in the dim light of the corridor a tall thin-faced man of about forty with bleak eyes and a chicken neck and a piece in his hand that even in poor light I recognized as a Colt .44 Magnum. He entered quickly with the pistol trained on my navel and I let my eyes widen in only half pretended fear and backed awkwardly into the living room. A second man, shorter and more compactly built and carrying a Woolite bottle in his hand, came into the suite and secured the door behind him. I kept retreating from Ordway and his Magnum, into the darkest corner of the living room, and unasked I faced the wall and assumed the standard frisk position. If the bottle man remembered my face as I had remembered his voice, my life was over. I twisted my neck around to watch as much of the room as possible. The bottle man came over to the wall I was leaning against and fumbled with the base of the fat-bellied lamp on a square mahogany table.

"Wife and kid in there?" Ordway nodded toward the closed door to the bedroom.

"Leave—leave them alone. Pl-please." I whined like a terrified victim of random crime and hoped the voice distortion would help keep the bottle man from remembering. "I'll give you everything I have if you don't hurt—"

The bottle man found the switch and the light from the table lamp hit my face and his own. The high forehead and the hooded look around the eyes were the same, but the nose looked bent and the mustache was gone and the plastic surgery scars gleamed dully in the lamp-glow. I hadn't seen that face in six years. The last time I'd seen it I had changed it. Until a few minutes ago I had never expected to see it again.

He was calling himself Merton Grandell now and running a kill-for-hire service under the cover of an organization that located missing heirs, but it was Max Gantry. I remembered the Jock had told me that he'd begun as an estate attorney in California but had gotten greedy and been disbarred. However he'd managed to square himself with Angelo Garza after the disaster to his money laundry, he'd wound up finding a new way to cash in on his knowledge of probate law. He saw me with my palms flat against the wall and his mouth went loose and his eyes danced as they had six years before in the

Ninth Street apartment of Mr. Gilbert Dann and he began to shake the liquid-filled Woolite bottle in his hand and at that moment I saw what every philosopher I had ever read had assured me was inconceivable. I saw myself dead. The wild man in my head thought about rushing him and wrapping my hands around his neck and strangling him while the Magnum tore holes in me.

It was Ordway who saved us both. When he saw Gantry's epileptic fit of facial contortions he understood without need for words that somehow in the last ten seconds everything had gone haywire. With his eyes and pistol still leveled on me he closed in on Gantry and slapped him across the cheek with his free hand. "What the Christ is wrong with you?" he hissed.

The smack and the words yanked Gantry back into reality like a bucket of cold water in the snoot. "I know this bastard," he said quietly. "He tried to take me in New York back in seventy-six. I owe him the roughest death anyone ever died."

"We have to stick to the plan," Ordway argued.

"Fuck the plan! The plan is shit! I don't know who this son-of-a-bitch is, but he sure as hell isn't the father of Ann Haskell's kid. This is some kind of scam. It's the goddamn broad's fault. I'll fix her face for it when we're out of here. But there's something I've gotta do before we vanish outta this hotel." He set the bottle down on the lamp table and spun me around to face him. "Hey, fuckface, here's a Matchwit Club riddle for you. What does a piece of bread feel like when it gets popped into the toaster? Don't know, huh? Well, you're about to find out." He slithered away from me and picked up and uncapped the bottle and released the reek of raw gasoline and went to the couch and saturated the cushions and recapped the empty bottle and tossed it into the hallway near the front door. His eyes were jerking again as he came within six feet of me and beckoned for me to cross the room. "Come on, god damn it, lie on the couch face down and drink some Super Unleaded. *Move!*" It was Gantry Furioso all over again, almost a replay of the scene in the Village six years ago when I'd changed his face. "Al," he ordered, "hand me the matches."

"I don't want any part of this," Ordway told him. "Come on, let's just shoot this clown and run."

"*No!* If you won't help then fuck you too, I'll do it myself. This is a class hotel, they put a couple books of matches in every room. You got yours from the dresser drawer in 906, right? So they gotta be here too, right?" The old Matchwit Club style of asking questions. I almost giggled. "You keep him covered. I'm gonna look."

Those were the words that convinced me I had a friend in high places. I could feel my heart drumming with excitement and pure terror. Look in the bedroom first, I begged him silently, *for the love of God look in the bedroom first.*

Gantry backed away with his eyes darting around the living room for a table drawer that might hold matches, and then seeing nothing likely he crossed to the bedroom door and flung it open. Once inside the doorway he was beyond my vision and I had to imagine what was happening in there. Ordway's face wore that trapped look. He kept the Magnum on my middle and I could feel him wrestling with the urge to force the issue, shoot me where I stood, and hustle Gantry out of there. From the bedroom I heard the clatter of drawers being opened and rudely slammed shut. I counted seconds and watched Ordway's trigger finger like a bird watching a snake and waited waited waited for another sound that I couldn't describe but would know sure as death when it came.

And then it did.

Crash of furniture. Roar of animal rage. High scream of unbearable agony. Ordway couldn't help himself, he turned his back on me and spun around facing the bedroom door in a combat crouch with the Magnum trained on the opening. They came at him, the two of them bursting through into the living room, clinging and snarling and shrieking and flailing, locked in an orgiastic death dance. Ordway threw himself out of their path and fumbled the Magnum. I stood in the corner paralyzed with my eyes bugging out and watched hypnotized as they writhed around and around together bound. Max Gantry and my bedroom backup man, Saltus Tebbs, alias Moose Eliot, the deformed giant Gantry had tortured and left for dead in the woods six years ago. Saltus's fright wig was bunched over the place where his ear should have been and he had Gantry bear-hugged against him with his left arm and his huge right paw was around Gantry's neck and forcing it back and back while he kneed him in the groin and roared like a wounded lion in his face. One of Gantry's arms hung limp and useless, half out of its socket. They bounded across the room and toppled onto the gasoline-soaked couch with Saltus's three hundred pounds crushing Gantry and his monster hands pressing the killer's nose and mouth into the black gunk. My body was starting to obey orders again. I swept the lamp off the heavy mahogany table and the room was in half darkness as Ordway found his fumbled Magnum on the carpet and shot into the pair locked like lovers on the couch. I had counted on the loss of lamplight to screw up his aim but the damn fool was so eaten by panic he didn't bother to aim, just pumped slugs wildly into the fabric and the two men. One of the bullets must have hit a steel spring and made a spark because suddenly there was a *whoom* and the couch and men were a screaming bloody inferno and the stench of cordite and roasting flesh was sickening. I heard shouts and pounding kicking noises outside in the corridor. Ordway was too stunned to hear anything. His back was still turned to me. I grabbed the lamp table by two legs and rammed it into the back of his neck. He sprawled forward and his hands clawed out for support and caught at the burning arm of the couch and he shrieked in pain. I gave him no mercy. Tore a leg off the sturdy table and clubbed him again and again on the head and face and neck and back, panting and babbling rage sounds and hearing the dull boom of shots and kicks somewhere behind me and then out of a corner of my eye seeing a small army of men bursting into the room and pulling me off Ordway and swatting at the couch and the burning men with jackets and soaked bath towels from the john and bed sheets and whatever else came to hand. I lay sprawled and hyperventilating in a corner, making noises that weren't human. Just before blackness fell like a guillotine blade I saw Zwack's face peering down at me.

FIFTEEN

The people with the fullest understanding of the world tend to be the ones who most appreciate a well-crafted sentence or a well-crafted story. The reason why this is so is not far to seek. The good sentence and the good story have structure, balance, direction; in short, all the wonderful assurances that life denies us.

Most of us anyway.

From the notebooks of Milo Turner

They shot dope into me and strapped me on a gurney and wheeled me out of the Centurion Inn into a bedlam of police cars with dome lights whirling and fire engines with sirens screaming and people in uniforms running in and people in various stages of undress running out like beheaded chickens. They stowed me in a boxy EMS vehicle with the orange stripe around its middle plain as daylight in the glare of portable floods and the next thing I knew I was in a shorty gown with a metal tag on my wrist and feeling cool white sheets under me and wrinkling my nose at the smells of disinfectant and slow dying that cling to every hospital in the world. I screwed my eyes shut and opened them again and raised my wrist to my eyes to read the name tag and find out who

I was this morning or evening or whenever. LATTMAN, ARTHUR, the letters read.

A burly black cop with sergeant's stripes on his uniform sleeves hoisted himself out of the dinky visitor's chair and crossed to the bed and bared gleaming choppers in a grin that would have lightened Scrooge's heart. "You okay, man?" His voice was deep with a built-in music all its own, and I guessed that his roots were in the West Indies. "How's it feel being a hero?"

I forced my eyes shut again, desperate for a few seconds to figure the situation. I didn't think I was under arrest. The sergeant sounded perfectly sincere, but for the life of me I couldn't make a particle of sense out of his calling me a hero.

"What time is it?" I muttered weakly.

"Little after ten."

"In the morning?"

"Ten P.M., man. You slept close to eighteen hours."

"God," I said stupidly.

"Lotta headlines while you've been out. Your boss is what they call the man of the hour. Front page spread in the *Globe* and the *Post* plus a couple minutes on the national news this evening, an interview on *Nightline* tonight, pieces for sure in the next *Time* and *Newsweek* . . ."

"My boss?" I had begun to realize that having emerged from one kind of fog I was already in the thick of another. "Luther Zwack?"

"Who else? I tell you, man, him and the fat cats in the department truly played this one close to their vests, but what a payoff! Chicago cops are going through the files in Grandell's office and, what I hear, they already found enough to connect him with seventeen murders all over the country that passed for accidents. The people that hired his agency to waste their relatives are getting picked up and invited down for questioning. Lawyers'll sure God get fat on all the trials come out of it. Couldn't have happened without you and Mr. Zwack and that big cat Tebbs."

"Tebbs." I didn't want to hear that name because it made me remember how he looked the last time I saw him. "Did he make it?"

"Sorry, man," the sergeant said softly. "He was DOA, like Grandell. The other hit guy's even worse off. Docs are saying his neck and back are broke, he'll be a quadriplegic the rest of his life. Ain't no court gonna reverse that judgment, man. You, uh, think you up to talkin' to the colonel yet?"

I dreaded having to face the top cops of Saint Louis County and to explain the whole mess without blowing my identity as Lattman the Manhattan Eye, but the timing happened to work in my favor. The superintendent of police, Colonel Lawrence, sat in the dinky visitor's chair with three of his senior aides standing around my bed while the five of us glued our peepers to the TV bracketed to the wall and watched Zwack being interviewed on a remote hookup and spelling out for *Nightline*'s Ted Koppel and incidentally for me the gist of the scenario. It was the onstage Zwack in full regalia, leprechaun grins and drawn-out we-e-ells and all. I was amazed he didn't gulp down bran on camera and even more amazed that there was so much truth in his lies. He explained that in professional discussions with his out-of-town colleague Arthur Lattman he had chanced upon the trail of what he soon began to suspect was a well-organized murder-for-hire ring that had been operating undetected for years. He and Lattman had worked out a scam to sucker the hit men into making an attempt on a certain Blake family, which in reality was Lattman and two assistants. Zwack's operatives plus a hefty contingent of cops were waiting in the wings to grab the killers with their pants down. The plan had been a magnificent success except for the tragic death of ace investigator Saltus Tebbs while trying to subdue the pair of assassins.

The segment gave me all the material I needed to play my part. Any holes in my account would be attributed to the lingering effects of my ordeal. Having been handed the case of a lifetime plus media kudos in abundance, these cops were in no mood to be hypercritical. They questioned me only till dawn. I will spare the reader a mountain of redundant dialogue and restrict myself to the part where we talked about arresting the person who'd hired Estates Investigative Services to murder Ann Haskell.

"You picked up Jeffrey today, didn't you?"

Colonel Lawrence looked at me blank-faced. "The dead woman's brother? Why in the world would we arrest him?" Then he understood and became my ally again. "I guess being doped up all day you couldn't have known." And, sitting Eisenhower-style on the flimsy chair with his elbows propped on its top edge, he told me what had happened.

Shortly before eight that morning a male and a female plainclothes detective had knocked on the door of a unit on the top floor of a luxury condominium building in West County with a warrant in their hands for the arrest of the unit's owner. As soon as Daria Shore saw them in the doorway she knew. Her eyes went dead, just like that. The TV in her front room was tuned to a morning newscast, so she must have been expecting the visit. She asked for a minute to use the john and spun around gracefully and ran across the apartment to a door at the far end that opened on the balcony and before the detectives could reach her she had swan-dived into the hot bright air and smacked the street seventeen stories below, tying up traffic for most of the morning.

So it was over. I'd been after the wrong person from the start, but as fate or luck would have it the right person had paid the bill at the end. Now I knew what Gantry had meant when he said., It's the goddamn broad's fault. "Jesus," I said. "No, I had no idea it was Shore. How—how did you know she was the one?"

"It was Zwack's idea," the colonel told me. "Don't ask me what gave him the notion, but he suggested that we ought to show a photo of her to the registration clerk at the Centurion. Sure enough, the guy identified her as the woman who'd checked into 906 with Ordway, as Mrs. Kenneth Holland. Well, we don't have to prove it in court now but the picture's pretty clear. While old Bradford Haskell was still alive, Shore made a deal with Grandell to kill Jeffrey, her future brother-in-law. That way, when the old man died her boyfriend Gene the fiddler would take the whole residuary estate. Or so she figured at the time. Then Ann the long-lost sister showed up and Shore decided to switch targets and told Grandell to take her out instead. She was the one who recommended that Jeffrey hire Estates Services to shadow Ann in New York. She set up the appointment between Jeff and Ordway. Then out of the blue old Bradford had another heart seizure and died."

"But being a lawyer," I said, "Shore knew she still had one hundred twenty hours to kill Ann and cut her out of the estate."

"Right. We know how Ordway did it. I've been on the phone with the New York cop in charge of that investigation, a kid named Dimjan or something. I'll bet he fell out of his chair when I told him the poor woman was murdered."

"Then Jeff's trip to New York right afterward was just what it looked like on the surface," I said. "A flying visit to help wind up his half sister's estate. God, I was blind! Once I learned that Shore was a lawyer too, and saw at that conference in Haskell's office how she had Gene wrapped around her little finger, I should have realized that for all practical purposes she had the same motive to kill Ann as the brothers had. She knew he'd marry her whenever she said the word. Eventually she'd have killed both brothers, or had Grandell do it for her, and wound up with most of the Haskell property for herself."

"You saved Jeff's life and Gene's life, plus God knows how many people in that hotel, plus whatever other people Grandell had contracted to kill. Good night's work, Lattman. Except for that poor devil Tebbs."

"Yeah." I tried not to think about Saltus with his fright wig and his missing ear. "But I'll tell you one thing that may make you feel a little better."

"What's that?"

"Hard as he died," I said, "I think he died content."

There was no way of avoiding the media. Too many ladies and gentlemen from too many newspapers and magazines and radio and TV stations were craving to grill Mr. Arthur Lattman. I spent most of the daylight hours in my hospital bed, catching up on sleep and going over my version of events and rehearsing answers to likely questions. At five that afternoon I held a news conference in a lounge on the main floor. I read a statement, allowed them half an hour for cross-examination that proved to be far from rigorous— I do not boast when I say they never laid a glove on me—then pleaded exhaustion and called a halt. The chief administrator of the hospital let me hide in his office while his paper-pushers processed my discharge. A little after nine, with the sun going down in an orgiastic orange haze, I slipped out through the swing doors of the emergency room and crossed the parking lot to the dark blue gas guzzler waiting by prearrangement in a far corner. Zwack himself was behind the wheel, wearing one of those denim leisure suits and a cat-with-cream expression. My suitcases were in the back of the car. He handed me an airline ticket as I settled into the passenger seat beside him.

"We have ninety minutes before it takes off," he said, "if you want to talk."

"What do you want me to say? God damn you, Zwack, you worked a scam on me! You took my money and agreed this operation would be private and then you brought in the cops. Between their digging and the media's I've only got a fifty fifty chance of coming out of this mess without being exposed as Milo Turner. And that's if I'm lucky!"

"You won't be exposed," Zwack said. "By day after tomorrow most of the newspeople will have just the vaguest recollection of who Arthur Lattman ever was. Don't you know what's been going down today?"

"I wasn't watching newscasts in there," I admitted.

"The number of murders linked to Grandell's organization has risen to twenty-two, including some ostensible accidents in extremely prominent and newsworthy families. Not only that, but it seems that Estates Investigative Services had a heavy Mafia connection. Half the company's profits wound up on the books of some businesses owned by Angelo Garza's branch of the Family back east."

"Garza," I repeated. "That explains what happened after the laundry operation fell through. Gantry talked his way out of trouble. Persuaded Garza to spread the word that he'd wasted Gantry, set up shop in Chicago as Merton Grandell, and repaid Garza for the money he'd lost by giving him half the take from his kill-for-hire setup."

"Angelo's never been convicted of anything before," Zwack said. "This time I think he will be. . . . Turner, you have to admit that once I realized how huge this deal was I had to go to the law."

"Which reminds me. How *did* you find out so much?"

"We-e-ell, I suppose it began when we had that long lunch downtown and you told me about the hundred-twenty-hour rule. It aroused the criminal side of me. I asked myself, Could this be the only instance of a legatee paying to have a relative killed so as to increase his own share of some estate? And that question aroused the entrepreneur in me, and I asked myself, What if there were a business that specialized in killings of that sort? So I had my research people sniff around for any accidental deaths during the past few years that resulted in drastic redistributions of any large estate, and the name of Estates Investigative Services kept popping up. Finally I took my dear friend Colonel Lawrence to lunch and we formed a sort of task force over our meal. Unorthodox but effective."

"And for the next few years," I said, "no one in Middle America will be able to think PI without thinking Luther Zwack. How nice for you."

"You needn't insult me. Just remember that Arthur Lattman's stock in the investigative world has gone through the roof too. You come out of this scam with all the revenge you wanted plus a ton of proof whenever you care to use it that you're one of the top private dicks in the country. I ought to surcharge you for the extra benefits but actually I've torn up your bill."

"How come the sudden burst of generosity?"

"I had a long talk with the Haskell brothers this afternoon. They are now firmly convinced that I saved their lives and are willing to reimburse both of us for all our expenses plus a handsome bonus. Naturally you'll have to dismiss that phony claim for a third of their father's residuary."

"Done," I said. "Poor Keel, there goes his big case. . . .

By the way, Colonel Lawrence told me it was your idea to show Daria Shore's picture to the registration clerk at the Centurion. What made you suspect she was the one who hired Grandell?"

"That woman who checked in with Ordway bewildered me. Estates Investigative Services has no woman operatives, and the notion that Mrs. Kenneth Holland was Grandell himself in drag was ridiculous. So I thought about the women connected with the Haskells and realized quickly that Shore had almost as strong a motive for disposing of your lady as the brothers did. Now that she and Grandell are dead we can't know for sure why she checked in with him, but obviously it wasn't her idea. When she went to Grandell and hired him to kill the child, I assume as a condition of the job he made her play an active part so she couldn't betray him later." He touched the dome light button and read his wristwatch. "I suppose we should start for Lambert. I think you'll want to make a phone call before you fly east."

"What gives you that idea?"

He dug into his pocket and handed me a pile of message slips, each bearing the same number, which I recognized at once. "She still accepts you as Lattman," he said as he twisted the ignition key and spun the guzzler out of the hospital zone. "I told her you were all right and would call her as soon as possible."

"Zwack," I said, "you're a bigger con artist than I ever was. It's a shame you gave up the life."

"We-e-ell," he said, "*I've* always considered it a lateral transfer."

I made two long-distance calls at the airport before I boarded the nonstop to LaGuardia. The second was to the Jock. I hadn't talked to him the whole time I'd been in Saint Louis, but he'd already familiarized himself with most of the story thanks to all the media coverage and our dialogue was not inordinately verbose.

"So," he murmured when I was through. "Both the Haskells were innocent as lambs. Ye know, me buck, way back when ye launched the grand scam I had a feeling they might be and tried to make ye see that there were other possibilities."

"You were right all the way," I confessed. "The grief screwed me up from square one. I kept thinking it was behind me and I was my old self again but I never was. Maybe I never will be again. I've been thinking about that today."

"But ye must be feeling on top of the world, I suppose," he said, "because vengeance was sweet."

"Wrong," I told him. "I've rarely felt lousier. It's as if I'm all empty inside. Drained. Sort of dead."

"I knew that would come," he said softly, "but ye wouldn't have believed me if I'd told ye. The fever had to run its course."

"Jocko, do you know what the Jews say about death?"

"No doubt something more sensible than most of me own countrymen say."

"They don't put much stock in immortality. When you're dead, you don't come back or rise again. But you're not really dead until the last person with living memories of you is dead too. Jock, I've been through hundreds of identities in my time, but . . . but she was the only one who knew there was a real me behind all the masks. Now that she's gone and I don't have revenge to sustain me I'm not sure I'm alive anymore."

I hadn't asked him a question and didn't expect any answer, but there was a long silence at his end, much longer than when he was faced with a simple challenge like giving me the name of a forty-five-year-old locomotive engineer of Serbo-Croatian ancestry who has lived in Keokuk, Iowa and is allergic to onions. I was almost ready to hang up the phone and check in at my plane's departure gate when his voice came back.

"Listen to the old fool, me lad," he said. "When the tag ends of this dirty business are behind ye, find a remote and hospitable place and stay there for a while. Sip wine. Update your memoirs. Let the emotions settle. Take a year if ye must, but if and when ye return to the life, come back whole."

"I'll think about it," I told him. "Gotta run now and catch my plane. . . . Thanks much, Jocko."

The flight through silky darkness with the cloud banks beneath the wide-body a soft gray in the moonlight gave me two and a half hours to empty my mind of everything but what was going to happen when I landed. I thought about how, just before I confided in Suzy as much of the story as I'd planned to tell, one of my voices had whispered to me that this woman is the right one. I remembered Joanne asking could I be her father all the time and the way it had given me a tremor of fright. In imagination I ran my hands gently down Suzy's lean strong sweet body as I had after the explosion of sexual release we had both needed so much. Dear God, how could I ever tell her the truth about me? And even if I could and did and it didn't make her hate me, how would we live? I could never ask her and the child to share the impossible multiple lives I'd carved out for myself. Did I want and need them enough to shut down those identities and settle into a pattern of living like other people? It wouldn't be the same as the retirement I had contemplated a few months ago. That lady and I had common roots, both of us sprung from the King Fox. Suzy was an alien, she'd never understand. Then again maybe she would. Hadn't she said she felt a rush of creativity pretending to be someone else? I could tell her everything tonight or tomorrow and gamble on her response or I could carry on as Arthur Lattman, enjoy a splendid reunion with her and then follow the Jock's advice and drift away into an obscure corner of the universe for a long recuperation.

The wide-body touched down and taxied across tarmac to its gate. I unfastened my seat belt and walked slowly up the aisle of the plane and along the Jetway ramp and through LaGuardia's corridors and then I saw the two of them running joyously toward me hand in hand like my own future and I froze and almost turned my back and ran away from them but kept standing there numb and waiting and frantically hoping that they would vanish in a magical puff of smoke and save me from having to make the toughest choice of my life. In silent desperation I begged one of my voices to tell me what in the hell to do.